FINDERS
WEEPERS

FINDERS
WEEPERS

Katie Letcher Lyle

Coward, McCann & Geoghegan, Inc.
New York

Library of Congress Cataloging in Publication Data
Lyle, Katie Letcher,   Finders weepers.
Summary: During a visit to the home of her
dying grandmother in the Blue Ridge Mountains,
Lee happens on a famous lost treasure which may
prove unlucky for herself as well as for others.
[1. Buried treasure—Fiction. 2. Blue Ridge
Mountains—Fiction. 3. Grandmothers—Fiction] I. Title.
PZ7.L9797Fi   [Fic]   82-1469
ISBN 0-698-20556-1   AACR2

For my father,
John Seymour Letcher,
and all his grandchildren:
Cochran and Jennie Lyle
Annie and Jamie Borda
Lucy, Susan, and Alice Letcher

PART I

There's gold, and it's haunting and haunting;
It's luring me on as of old . . .

—"The Spell of the Yukon"
Robert Service

Thursday, June 1

1

WHEN I FINALLY GET A MINUTE TO MYSELF AND MAKE IT TO THE back porch, it's almost six. Earlier I had to hang up on my friend Barbara when Drew, trying to zip his pants up, knocked into the toilet seat and it fell and bonked him on the head and he started to cry. I had to keep him quiet because Mama was resting, and I never got a chance to even call Barbara back. But Gee and I got a good start on his tree house today while Drew took his nap. Now late sun tints the letter I've been trying to read a faint gold. Which is just the color I figure this letter ought to be, since it's from my uncle Graham Eldridge, Graham the Great. He's my happy-go-lucky uncle, the black sheep of the family, that's according to Daddy.

Inside the house, in the background, life goes on: the smell of supper cooking, the clang of one pan against another, Andrew and Green fighting. It's my first day out of school, and I couldn't even get away to meet Barbara and Camille at the drugstore. What was I so excited about all winter, just waiting to get out for vacation? I wipe perspiration off my face and wonder what July's going to be like with the first of June this hot.

The kids are tired because it's what Graham calls low-blood-sugar time and Mama has principles about eating between meals.

"If you won't give it to me, you can't ever play with my cards again!" Green, usually the patient one, sounds really angry. I hope supper will be ready soon. I guess I should go offer to help.

"I won't I won't I *won't!*" Andrew's baby voice demands to be heard, ending in a long quivering wail.

"Lee will make you!" cries Gee, old enough that his threats sound effective. Again Drew wails.

On the porch steps, I sigh, drawn into their bouts even with my body in another room! If Mama would just give them a snack about five, they'd be okay until supper. But she just says, "I don't know why they have to fight all the time."

"They don't," I tell her. "Just when they're cross and tired and hungry. It only happens at the end of the day. You could just give them a banana or something."

She's big on Eating the Right Things, but that doesn't grab her. "They wouldn't eat a bite for supper. Bananas are very filling. Besides, I'm not running a short-order café. Now get out of my hair, Miss Sensible, so I can drain these potatoes." She takes a sip of her old-fashioned, drags out an orange section, skins it down and consumes it. Maybe that doesn't count as eating. She usually has her drink before Daddy gets home, so as to avoid as much as possible his harangues about her drinking. He makes it sound as if she's an alcoholic.

I suppose Drew and Green will survive their childhoods. You could say I did.

But Graham's letter, heavy with possibility, is waiting to be read, and already I can hear his voice, always excited and exciting, bigger than life. Someday Graham is going to take me to Europe. Someday he's going to buy me a fur coat. He's already taken me to a bar, though Mama and Daddy don't know, needless to say. He thinks I need a horse of my own to ride. (When he told Daddy that at Christmas, it infuriated Daddy, who thinks you ought not to *spoil* kids.) With Graham I drank champagne one time last year until I was a little dizzy.

But this time the letter is different. I find a frightening note in the first sentence, and quickly take off my glasses and breathe on them and yank out a shirttail to wipe them clean before I put them back on. Now my eyes trip along the lines of Graham's rather dainty writing, trying to absorb everything at once, for the first sentence says, "Honey, I don't at all mean to alarm you—I'm writing to Hy and Kate too—but Malillie has had a mild stroke."

Now my vision scatters wildly, tumbling over words: ". . . not too severe . . . the doctor says . . . business is slow at the store . . . a nurse is out of the ques-tion . . . Bessie is so old now . . . only comes a couple of hours . . . now you're out of school, you'd be such a help . . . always so responsible . . .

". . . So you made it through the eighth grade! want to give you a graduation present, but will wait to see what you need . . . high heel shoes?

"Hope you will come, and soon . . . Malillie loves you so . . ."

Inside the house, Mama cries out, "Drew! Put that knife down this instant! Do you want to cut your hand off?" And Drew begins to wail mournfully.

"Leeeee?"A voice comes through the screen, so close I can feel the hot breath carrying it. "I need to show you something."

"In a second, Drew," I tell him. "Let me finish Graham's letter."

"It's a baby elephant," Drew says. "A real one. It's for you."

I look up and can't help smiling. "But you already gave me a tiger, and a whale, today. Give the elephant to Mama. She *needs* an elephant."

Andrew frowns and shakes his head. "She has to cook. You know she doesn't like pets in the house. It's for you, Lee."

"Bring it here, then," I say, sighing, opening the screen door. My mind is already back on the letter. "Thanks very much."

Out he comes, stepping down a giant step, and tumbles into my lap, curling up immediately into a round body-fitting shape. He smells of dead dry grass and souring milk. "You need a bath," I say into his soft hair, thinking, Malillie, ill? Malillie is the strongest, best person I've ever known. She's pure gold. She is like nobody else in my life. She isn't very old, but she's fat. What's a mild stroke anyway? Certainly not too serious, or Graham would have called us up. She's not in a hospital, so it couldn't be too bad.

"Gosh, it's hot," I say aloud, wishing to be rid of the weight of the sticky little body of my brother hunkered down against mine. Around his soft head I struggle to reread the letter slowly, while Drew cautions me not to squeeze the elephant too tight. "See, he's just a baby!"

What does a mild stroke mean?

I am being asked to come. I go to see them every summer, but usually near the end of June, in time for Malillie's birth-

12

day on the twenty-seventh. I love to help with the canning and preserving and jelly-making. I've known the dates everything "comes in" since I was little: I miss the first wild strawberries around June 1, but I get there in time for everything else: blackcaps come in just about the time I get there, and wineberries July 10, and blackberries ten days later. The corn starts August 1, and then I have to go home usually before the huckleberries come in, late in August. Sometimes I stay in the store for Graham while he harvests the June apples or the peaches in the tiny orchard out back. I've been doing that since I was ten. I love running the store all by myself, and there's nothing to it.

That time, July and August, suits Mama, because Daddy takes his vacation and can help with the boys while I'm gone. Mama doesn't have much stamina, and often seems sort of swamped by her life. Sometimes she has to go away to a fancy hospital sort of place called Westwood for a few weeks to rest, and then I more or less run the whole house by myself. Will she be able to manage if I go to Lavesia?

In my lap, Drew stirs. "I'm hungry," he whines. "I wish I had a waffle."

"A waffle?" I say, giving him a little hug. "That's silly. You don't eat waffles for supper. How waffle!"

Drew sucks on his fingers.

"Don't do that, hon," I tell him. "Look how dirty they are. Listen, supper's almost ready. I'll make you waffles for breakfast tomorrow, okay?"

"With maple syrup?"

"Sure," I say.

"And butter?"

"Lots of butter. Melted butter."

"Don't let Gee have any," Drew says. "He's mean. *Mean Gee.*"

13

"Oh," I say, doing the best I can at mediation, "we wouldn't want Green to starve. Let's give him maybe just a little one, okay?"

"Well . . ." he says, hesitating.

Behind us, Green leans on the door. "Lee, after supper, would you ride bikes with me?" What he means is, he'd like to ride all the way to the club and pretend its big round driveway is the Indianapolis Speedway, and zoom around it until he's beat, while the people are all inside eating dinner. Without me, he's only allowed to go to the end of the street.

I smile up at him. "Okay, Gee. I guess so."

"Can I go too?" Drew asks, with big pitiful eyes.

"Honey," I say, "that's a little too far for you."

He puckers up. "I have to go," he wails. "You have to take me!"

Over the din, Mama calls, "Lee, can't you *do* something?" She means, to make them quit, for now Gee is saying, "You're too little. You're a baby. See, you're crying!"

Just then up the cement slab cruises a dusty blue Chevrolet, heavy and old. "Oh, look!" I shout, with exaggerated excitement. "Here comes Daddy. Daddy's home. Now we can eat!"

The car turns into the parking space. But before I can scrabble to my feet with the heavy baby on my lap, Daddy's voice shouts, "Lee, goddamn it, get these boards and junk out of the driveway before I run over them! Can't you *ever* put anything away?" And then I remember: Gee's tree house! Oh, no! I think. Now we'll have to listen to how irresponsible I am all through dinner. For a brief instant I have a vision: of wealth, of freedom, of grown-up-ness, of long sea voyages and beautiful clothes and palm trees and music. Oh, *when* will something happen to take me away from all this!

Monday, June 5

2

DADDY AND I ARE ON THE WAY TO LAVESIA, ME HOPEFUL THAT WE can maintain a pleasant atmosphere for the five-hour drive. When Mama waved us off, and I said, "Don't forget Gee's allergy medicine. Tell Drew I'll bring him something—" she just grinned and shook her head. "Who do you think you are, their *mother?* You give Lillie and Graham my love, you hear?" The diesel-exhaust smell of the city is behind us now. I have not drunk anything, as it irks Daddy to have to stop for me to go to the bathroom. He is already annoyed at having to take a day off from work to drive me, but plane fare to Roanoke was too expensive, and there is no other way. Graham taught me to drive last summer, but naturally Daddy doesn't know that.

It is a sad fact that I irritate Daddy. He expects children to act like grown-ups. He named me for his mother, and I agree with him that she's pretty near perfect, and I guess I'm just not. One time when he was mad at me about something when I was about eight, he said, "Why do you have to be so damned immature?" And *I* said, "But I'm only *eight*," and then he really did get mad.

And it's another sad fact, I guess, that I still knock myself out trying to do what I figure he wants me to do, things like building Gee a tree house. And it's never good enough. Either the thing falls down, or I forget to clean up after myself. If I want a new dress, I'm extravagant. When I wanted high heels, I was too young. Today won't be any different. Yet I've memorized a list of things to talk to him about, to avoid irritating subjects—things that will keep his mind off the fact that he has to spend a whole day with me. Mama tries to explain frequently that it isn't personal, it's just him.

Since he loves to talk about his childhood, I say, "Tell me about you and Graham and the goat." He chuckles to himself, and I can relax a little. The land is still flat and red, but the road goes straight west, lit up by the sun at our backs.

"Aw," he says, "that was one of Graham's great schemes to make money. One day a friend of his sold him a goat for two dollars. Said Graham and I could make eight dollars a week selling goat milk. Graham borrowed the money from me; he never could save any money. Said he'd pay me back the first week. Anyway, we took the goat home and while we were explaining this great plan to her, Mother came out back to see it. 'That's a fine idea,' she said, 'except for one thing.' 'What's that?' we asked. 'It's a billy goat,' she said." And Daddy gets red in the face laughing. "After that, whenever Graham had some big plan to make money, Mother would say, 'Remember the goat.' We liked to kill that boy—Robert Maguire his name was—next time we saw him. Later on, though, he went to the penitentiary for killing somebody over some moonshine whiskey."

Daddy's stories are all like that: rounded with retribution. "It's a billy goat," he repeats, in a kind of imitation of Malillie.

I chuckle appreciatively. "You all must have had a lot of fun," I say.

"We worked hard," he says. "Kids today don't work. At least *I* did." He means Graham didn't. He seems to be accusing me of not working, too.

"Oh, I know!" I say quickly. "I know you did."

"I'd like a nickel for every hour I put in at the loading platform and the storeroom at the hardware. We'd have been rich today if Lavesia had grown, like it was supposed to, after the second world war. *And* if Graham hadn't gone off half-cocked into some damnfool thing like *antiques*."

Quick, what's on my list that will get him off this track?

"Tell me about how you used to go looking for the Beale Treasure!"

And I slide a worried glance over at him to see whether I've managed to divert a harangue about Graham's extravagances, which would lead to *my* extravagances, since he often compares me to his brother, which would lead to his constant theme about how hard he works and how he just barely makes enough to get us from one payday to the next.

"The Beale Treasure!" he says, shaking his head. "God knows how many hours I spent looking for that. All of us did, except Graham. He never did believe the Beale Treasure existed."

"Well, I don't know," I say slowly, "but it seems to me, if you think about it, Mr. Beale supposedly hid it around there in 1822, which is a long time ago, and it was supposedly one heck of a lot of stuff. It just does seem like, if he *really* did, somebody would have found it by now, all the looking that goes on."

"You're just like Graham," he observes, right on cue.

I think for an instant fondly, protectively, of Graham. He's

17

not rich, but he doesn't have a wife and family, so he gets champagne, trips to New York, big cars. I don't mind if I'm like him. But it galls Daddy, who works hard and never has anything extra.

"He was always perverse as hell," Daddy goes on. "Whatever the rest believed, he'd believe the opposite, just for the devil of it. He never did take any stock in the treasure. Maybe he was right. He's never been right about much else."

I slant my eyes around, but he's squinting at the road. A zillion pine trees zip by, above shoulders of eroding clay.

"You still think it exists?" I ask.

"I don't think about it anymore," he says.

What else doesn't he think about anymore? What *does* he think about anymore, coming home tired every night, fighting with his boss, taking the boys fishing, then coming home mad because Gee wouldn't take the fish off the hook, or Drew fell out of the canoe, or something.

"Only time Graham ever did make money was once he got a notion to buy five-cent cigars and steal just enough of Pop's rum to dribble a little over them and give them a good rummy smell; then he sold them in the truck stop for fifteen cents apiece to the truckers all one summer. I went along because he'd give me a penny every cigar as long as I didn't tell. A penny bought considerable candy in those days. But someone ratted on us, and Pop licked us both. It wasn't selling the cigars that bothered him, it was stealing his rum." He laughs. "We used to smoke the cigars ourselves."

"You did?" I am amazed. Daddy is of the "lips that touch tobacco shall never touch mine" persuasion, with which I agree. He made Mama stop smoking when they got married. *And* painting her nails *and* going to the beauty parlor. In fact, I worry about Graham, who still smokes little fragrant cigars all the time.

But Daddy's looking at me in a funny way. "Don't act so shocked," he says. "George Slatter told me he saw you smoking with some of your friends the other day in the drugstore."

It's my turn to stare at him. "That's not true," I say. "It wasn't me."

I wait for him to nod, or laugh, or give some sign that he knows, that he understands that nosy old George, the neighborhood troublemaker, has made a mistake at best, or at worst, has lied to get me in trouble. "What did you tell him?" I ask.

"Nothing. He just thought I ought to know."

"But, Daddy, you *know* how I feel about smoking."

He doesn't reply.

I feel a surge of anger. "*Don't* you know how I feel about smoking?"

He shrugs, which makes me madder.

"*Don't* you know it couldn't have been me?" I'm trying not to shout.

"Watch your tone of voice, young lady," he warns.

But I go on. "We have lived in the same house all my life," I say, feeling hotter than a Franklin stove. "Did I ever smoke?"

"Then why are you getting so upset?" he asks.

"Because that's insane, to think I—"

"Insane?"

"Yes. I don't understand why you can't see that!"

"Well, I'm sorry I told you." Now he's getting angry. He doesn't understand.

"Why didn't you take up for me?" I ask.

"All kids smoke these days."

"*But you know that I don't!*"

"You're sure being touchy as hell about it," he observes.

19

In fact, he doesn't know a damn thing about me.

I take off my glasses to rest my eyes. I will think of Lavesia, where life seems to have slowed to about half the usual rpm's. Immediately the landscape blurs into a bluish green made of trees and sky, a gap of open land, then more trees blurring into more dark land. I can't see worth a hoot without my glasses, but sometimes I think the world looks better when you can't see too well. It amazes me that the world can contain both Norfolk and Lavesia, only a few hours apart by time-travel, but centuries apart, really. Whole philosophies apart. In Malillie's lovely messy kitchen, I will bake and pickle and preserve all summer, and raise wonderful odors that no one will complain about.

I wondered about bringing the boys, or just Andrew, but Daddy doesn't know how sick his mother is. And if I had to take care of Andrew, I couldn't help Malillie.

When we did *Brigadoon* at school last winter, and I was in the chorus, I wrote to Malillie and Graham about how Brigadoon reminded me of Lavesia. In *Brigadoon,* a town appears out of the fog for only one day every one hundred years, so there's not much room for change and modernization. Lavesia has always felt like someplace from another century, connected to the rest of life only by this highway, Route 60, that each summer takes me there past green farms, miles and miles of forest, and tiny towns, lifting me gently higher and higher above sea level, into the Blue Ridge Mountains. Maybe the boys will come someday, but not yet. I didn't come until I was six, the year before Green was born.

Take Hunter. Even he is like somebody out of a book. He's my only friend my age in Lavesia. When he was a little boy, he threw eggs at the train when it passed through his father's farm. I couldn't figure it, because he was so gentle to

20

animals and people. Then later I realized he didn't like modern things, and that train must have seemed modern to him. I asked him about that last summer, and he was embarrassed. Hunter is different from the boys I know at home.

It always seems to me that somewhere on this concrete ribbon of road is a time warp, some secret, enchanted spot that no mortal eye can determine, a magic line that zips you unknowing a hundred years back in time.

Once I counted, and Lavesia has only thirty-four real houses, thirty-five if you count ours, a mile up the mountain from town. The bike ride in is always terrific, downhill the entire way. I always think it would be a wonderful sled ride in winter, and someday I'll come in the winter and try it. Maybe all of us will.

Daddy fiddles with the radio buttons, snapping from one station to another, playing static like it was an instrument. He gets dentist-office music for a while; then it blurs as we drive out of range.

He snaps the radio to off, and the road crackles under our tires. "I don't know what shape Mother is in," he says suddenly, "but don't be getting any ideas you're here for a vacation. You can do the cooking, and look after her. You let Graham look after the store." Is this to punish me for talking back earlier?

I can't help it; I feel anger rising in my body like a flood tide. It's not as if I'm irresponsible. For years I've taken care of my younger brothers, done the housework, and even done the shopping and the cooking for all of us while Mama's been sick. I make straight As. One time when I got 99 on a history test, Daddy actually said, "What happened? Weren't they giving out any hundreds today?" Never a word of praise, or thanks. He doesn't trust me, never has, and I spend my life

21

trying to be trustworthy. Goddamn! I swallow. I don't want a fight in the car like this, but I have my principles. I weigh my words with care: "I'll do whatever Malillie and Graham want me to. You don't have to worry."

But that's not good enough. "You listen to what I'm telling you. You got no business trying to run a store at your age. And Graham's got no business to let you."

I should just say yes and let it go, but I can't help it. "Jerry Dunne is right across the street if I need anything."

"Jerry Dunne is a confounded morphodyke. You stay away from him."

"He's a *what?*"

Daddy swallows and his face blushes red as if burned by fire. "A morphodyke. They call them dykes. For short."

I don't say anything. I feel embarrassed and uncomfortable, so I shut up. I'll put it on my list. I spell it to myself, trying to memorize it. It must be something terrible. I mean to look it up.

Our climb toward the bluish haze of the mountains has been nearly imperceptible. All morning sunlight has beamed down, then faded, graying the landscape, rolling across us like waves as clouds pile up in the sky ahead of us over the mountains. We pass signs from time to time that remind me of my hunger. I'm so thirsty I could drink a Coke, and I can't stand Cokes. ANY SAND CHIP DRINK $2.49, reads a billboard. HOSTESS INN 4 MILES says another, HOME-COOKED FOOD. Before us, the eastern slope of the Blue Ridge looms finally, changing color in the changing morning light from purple to gray or green to blue, the colors of the sea water that once stood where we now drive.

Think of Lavesia, I instruct myself. Cool down. Try to see his point of view. But instead I think of how Malillie and I

22

will stay up late playing canasta like always, of how whatever I decide for supper is what we'll have. I wonder what Hunter will be up to this summer. He's fifteen, two years older than me, and a couple of summers back his voice went up and down like there were two people inside him trying to talk at the same time. He works his father's farm in the summers by himself, ever since his father got emphysema, and helps out during the school year too. Every now and then he can get away to go swimming or caving. I usually see him on Saturday nights. Apparently Daddy hasn't remembered him.

As we begin the winding climb up the first mountain, rain spatters on the windshield, then blurs and darkens the road ahead. Daddy turns on the windshield wipers, and after a while, my ears begin to crackle.

"When we get there, I want to go in and talk to Mother alone," he says. I start to protest that I want to see her right away too, but I shut up, knowing it is no use. "I'll drop you by the store," he continues, "and you come on home later with Graham."

Count to twenty. Count to a hundred. A *million*. He won't ever consider my feelings, or include me—thinks I am some kind of a nitwit.

"What's a morphodyke anyway?" I ask, figuring it for my next word-of-the-week.

He clears his throat and again flushes bright red. "It's—a mixture—an unnatural mixture—you'll have to ask your mother about that," he says. Then he sounds very angry again. "You just stay away from him."

Stay away? *Cool it*, I instruct myself. When he goes, I can do what I please. Graham and Malillie love me. Hunter and Jerry Dunne and Bessie like me. What do I care about him?

23

3

THROUGH THE WET WINDSHIELD, GRAHAM'S FAMILIAR SIGN, OLD
gold lettering against wet black wood, says, ELDRIDGE'S
HDWRE, GEN. MDSE. The bottom line reads, EST. 1880.
Hanging beneath is the sign Graham added: purplish with
white lettering, it says THE WHITE ELEPHANT. Drew
would like that. What are Gee and Drew doing right now?
Will they be all right? Graham thinks I worry too much
about them.

"What an asinine goddamn name," Daddy says, not for the
first time. Graham took over the business when Grandaddy
couldn't do it any longer, but hardware went slow, and the
part Graham calls genmerdize (everything from shoepeg corn
to shoe pegs) went even slower. Graham couldn't compete
with the shopping centers developing near Roanoke and
Lynchburg, so gradually he'd phased out genmerdize, moved
hardware to the back, and added furniture, new and second-
hand, about the time I started coming. Diversifying, he called
it, and that was my first word-of-the-week.

People in these parts wanted things fixed more than they
wanted to buy new, so Graham started repairing furniture in
the old storeroom. That led him finally into antiques, or
junque, as he privately called it. And he changed the name to
The White Elephant. "See you later, Daddy," I say, getting
out onto the rainy street.

I push open the door, shaking rain off like a wet dog. The
sweet tinkle of the bell welcomes me back. I take off my
glasses and find a shirttail down under my sweater to wipe
away rain. Nobody.

I take a big breath of furniture oil, burlap, Scotch-gard, and wood. I zigzag back past a colonial bedroom and a Queen Anne dining room and a yellow modern kitchen, none of them with walls. Then I veer right, into the repair and antique shop.

It's as crowded as an attic: furniture old, new, broken, or half-fixed. On the floor are tools, shoes, books, sawdust, paper balls, boxes. In the filthy window is a bottle collection, everything from an old bubbled bluish one to a Heinz catsup, circa yesterday. An open box of doughnuts sprinkles powdered sugar onto a blue velvet sofa that teeters on top of a tractor.

Then my eyes find Graham. He's motionless, stretched in a Windsor chair upholstered in needlepoint vinery, its sides shredded by some cat's claws. Graham's long feet are propped on a leather daybed, and a bag of candy is in his lap. A dead cigar is on the chair arm. Daddy says Graham only keeps the store for something to do and a place to learn all the latest gossip. Green and Drew would go bananas in this room.

"You asleep?" I ask, softly, so as not to startle him.

"Just resting my eyes," he mumbles, automatically. Then he blinks and peers up through his bottle-bottoms that are maybe even thicker than mine, and sees it's me. "Aha!" he exclaims, struggling up. "Who is this vision of pure loveliness? You're enough to cure a hangover!"

"Graham!" I say, embarrassed.

"Haven't we met before?" he asks. "Let's see—Algiers, '55, wasn't it?" He reaches out his skinny arms, as if in yearning.

"You make more fuss," I say, loving it.

He slaps his shiny forehead. "Oh, no—what a mistake! It's only you, my favorite niece!"

25

When we hug I realize I have, over the winter, grown nearly as tall as Graham. He feels skinnier than ever. "Favorite? I
thought I was the only one."

"Does that keep you from being favorite?" he says. "Just
because you leave me no choice—don't you know that
freedom lies in the acceptance of necessity? Shakespeare,
Merchant of Venice."

"I'll bet," I say.

"Here, you gorgeous creature, have a malt ball."

"No, thanks. My figure."

Graham pops two in his mouth, and for a second looks
like a chipmunk. "Hell," he says, "you won't get fat. You're
cut out of the same cloth as me."

"So they say," I grin at him.

"Good thing we're both so good-looking," he says. "Me, I
don't want to waste away to nothing."

"How are you doing?" I ask.

"Hell, honey," he says, "if I looked as good as I feel,
I can tell you you'd be hugging Cary Grant. Hey!
Congratulations!"

"On what?" I ask. I skin my sweater over my head and
drop it onto a chair, and begin to sit. "I didn't *think* you had
it straight who I was."

"Hey, watch it!" he says, grabbing my arm. "Not that one.
It belonged to Edmonia Freeman. She was so mean, if she fell
into the James River, you'd go *upstream* to the rescue." He
pushes me toward another chair. The bottom falls through as
I sit. Graham gives me a scornful glance. "How many times
do I have to tell you, that isn't very funny—"

He sits again. "Miss Edmonia died last winter. They say
she shot herself, but I figure Seth did it. He'd been going with
a married woman for years. Seth Freeman brought that chair

in a week after the funeral. 'It's stained,' he tells me. 'Needs redoing,' he says. 'Grape juice.' But just look close, baby. Blood, if you ask me."

"Graham—" I want to ask about Malillie. And I want out of this chair frame.

But he ignores my waving arms. "Now let me see—where was I? Oh, yes—congratulations. Right. On *what*, you ask. Let's see. Well—on getting here early. Thought you weren't coming in until supper."

"Daddy has to get back. He's talking to Malillie now. I guess he needs to see how she's doing."

"Well," says Graham, still ignoring my plight, "on graduating from eighth grade, for another thing. If I recall correctly, eighth grade was just a little longer than anything else I ever endured. On being"—now he gets up and pretends to try to measure me with an invisible tape measure. I've given up, and remain folded in the chair frame—"at least seven and a half feet tall, not to mention absoloot-ly gorgeous. You *do* take after me! But you really need to do something about that posture." He eats a couple more balls of candy out of his bag. "You sure you don't want some?"

"Help," I say. So he hauls me out and hugs me again. It crosses my mind at this instant how weird my friends in Norfolk would find this scene. I begin to grin, thinking of it. There is no point where the two worlds touch. I smooth down my denim skirt.

"And last, but not least," he says, "for being named Most Sensible. Imagine that!"

"Oh, Graham! It's the dumbest award. The girl that got Most Likely to Succeed just wants to get married and have twelve children. How could anyone succeed with twelve children?"

Graham raises his eyebrows above his glasses. "If you did," he says, "that'd be real success."

"Well," I say, "me, I don't put any stock in those awards. Promise you won't say anything to anybody. I just told you because I thought you'd think it was funny."

Graham only laughs.

"Tell me," I say, "how Malillie is, *really.*"

He considers for a second. "Well, you can look at it two ways. For almost seventy-five and damn near blind, she's fantastic. On the other hand, she's slowing down, can't deny it." He brings out a new cigar, unwraps it, lights up.

I love talking with Graham, because he acts like I'm an adult, too. "What did the stroke do to her?"

He takes a big puff, blows it out so there's a sweet cloud of smoke between us. "You don't notice much—I just think she needs someone there during the day. She forgets to eat, for example. Or sometimes she puts on her nightgown in the middle of the morning. Things like that. Why does Hy want to see her alone?"

"He didn't tell me." The perfume from the cigar *does* smell like rum.

"How's he getting along? Are things any better with this new company?"

"He's fine."

"Is he treating *you* all right?"

"Sure," I say.

He rolls his eyes comically, and puffs on the cigar. "And how are Green and Andrew?"

"Growing like weeds," I say. "They're great. Typical little boys. Gee's dying for a dog, and a ten-speed. Drew's just snuggly. Listen. Are you telling me the whole truth about Malillie?"

28

"Course I am, honey. She's fine. She just needs a little company." And he smiles.

"You seen Hunter lately?"

"Sir Hunter the Upright? The Haloed One? That Hunter? He comes in to speak every so often. His father's the same, uses that cough of his as an excuse not to work. In February his ma came and brought us some maple syrup." Hunter is from a very religious family, the youngest of three boys. The others are married. None of them drinks, smokes, or swears, and, according to Graham, they go to church all day long every Sunday. Hunter's the only person I know anywhere near my own age in Lavesia, and not as bad as Graham makes out.

"Listen," I say, "Hunter just lives his religion, that's all. Not too many people do."

"That's true," Graham says. "Everyone's got to believe in something. I believe I'll have another malt ball." He abandons the cigar on the edge of a dresser.

I hear the doorbell tinkle. A loud crash follows. When we get there, a man lies sprawled just inside the door, half on top of a beat-up enamel gas stove. "Goddamn it," he says, "If she thinks—"

He sees us. "Help me up, Graham."

"What happened to that stove, Harold?" Graham hauls him to his knees.

"It's—semi-broke, that's what."

"Semi-broke? That anything like being semi-pregnant?" Graham winks slyly at me.

"Norma made me bring it. I told her it couldn't be fixed, and she said you'd fix it or else."

Graham stands there peering at the machine. "What in hell happened to it, Harold? Don't tell me—let me guess. It got hit by lightning."

29

"It got hit by me," Harold says, struggling to his feet. "Still works some. It just don't *look* so good."

"Hold it," Graham says. "You know my niece, Miss Lee Eldridge?"

The man nods in my direction. "Gladdameetcha," he mutters. "This damn stove been on the blink for more'n a year. Pilot won't stay lit. Eyes go out. Oven overheats. I do the cooking, see, and I'm damn tired of burning everything. Yesterday it burnt up two chess pies—" He glances at me, shamed, then at Graham. "I got mad, took a ax to it. Now Norma says I got to get it fixed."

Graham puts his hands on his hips. "Harold," he says, "let me sell you a new one."

"If I could afford a new one, I'd of bought it a long time ago," says Harold. The doorbell tinkles again, and I look up.

"Listen," Graham says, "I'll charge you as much as a new one to fix this one up. Then what'll you have? A fixed, beat-up old stove. That's what."

Harold shakes his head, refusing to be reasonable.

"You wouldn't have to pay for it all at once," Graham says. He holds out the bag of candy. "Have a malt ball?" Harold shakes his head again.

"I got a nice antique wood stove I can let you have—"

We have another customer. Immediately I know him for a treasure hunter: backpack, heavy boots, nylon jacket. This one isn't a caver; no ropes or lights. He has a beard as straggly as last year's asparagus, and a broken shovel.

"I help you?" Graham asks.

"Lissen," Harold mutters, "see what you can do. Norma wouldn't take to no wood stove."

"Hell, you're the one does the cooking," Graham says. But

30

Harold, with a nod at me, leaves, and the bell tinkles again.

"Shovel give out on you?" Graham asks.

"Can I get a new one from you?" the man wants to know. His eyes keep shifting over to the amazing wrecked stove lying in the aisle.

"No need," Graham says. "See that stove? Feller beat it up himself, now he wants me to fix it. I'll bet yours was at least an accident. Lookahere." He strides over to the wall, where bins stand full of all sizes and shapes of lumber. He goes on talking while he looks for a replacement handle.

"Tighter than a tick, that one. But right free when it comes to buying liquor. This won't take a minute. He has to keep it in the garage since his wife won't let him drink in the house. You want a malt ball?"

The man takes one, stares at it in his hand as though it's something he's never seen before. "Where are you planning to look?" I ask.

He grins. "All treasure hunters look alike, is that it?" I'm embarrassed, but he goes on. "I'm going to look right around Morriss's Tavern. See, I don't figure Beale hauled that much gold very far. I got a metal detector in the car." He eats the malt ball, popping and crunching it to death quickly. There are only two kinds of treasure hunters: they're very secret about where they plan to look, or they'll talk your ears off.

"Is Morriss's Tavern still around?" I ask, surprised I hadn't known.

"Nope," Graham says, whittling fast, curls of wood spiraling down onto the dark wood floor. "Burned down over a hundred years ago. Nobody seems to know where it was, anymore." He gives me a quick glance. "Some *claim* to know."

31

"I got a pretty good idea," the man says. "I put it in the computer."

"You really must believe in the Beale Treasure," I say, testing a yellow stool before sitting on it.

"Well, sure," he says, surprised. "Don't you?" He frowns and combs his fingers through his beard.

"I don't know. It doesn't seem too sensible, not after all this time."

"Better watch her," Graham says. "She was just named Most Sensible in her whole school. Not any dinky country school neither. Big consolidated school down in Norfolk. She's—"

"Graham!" I say. "I *asked* you not to—"

"Well, you were, weren't you?" he retorts.

It's useless to get mad. I reckon Graham couldn't keep still about a thing if his life depended on it.

"You've heard of heart transplants and liver transplants?" he asks, winking at me. "Well, I'm gonna get me a tongue transplant, then you won't have anything to worry about." He gives the handle a last whack. "Here you go," he says, handing it to the man. "Now don't go digging up the whole county, you hear?"

The man looks at the handle, pulls at it.

"Good as new," Graham says.

"Thanks," the man looks at me. "You've got a point, young lady, but I sure hope you're wrong." Now why couldn't Daddy talk like that to me? I don't want *agreement*, just politeness is all. Reason is my middle name, as Graham would say. "How much do I owe you?" the man asks Graham.

"A-ah—two dollars ought to do it. If you find Mr. Beale's treasure, you bring me a handful of gold dust."

"You bet," the man says. He pays and leaves. Graham lets

out a sigh like a big whoosh, and stuffs several malt balls into his cheek. He offers me the bag, but I still don't want any. "I'll never understand it," he says. "Grown men. They really think they're going to find all that loot and get rich." Together we laugh. "Everyone in the world's crazy but me and you, and sometimes I worry about you."

"I don't believe in it," I protest.

"Of course not. You're Most Sensible. You know what? If anyone ever did find it, it'd be nothing but trouble. For everyone. But I don't think we got a lot to worry about." He starts to work, pulling nails out of the sofa with the back of a hammer head. "Give me a deer hunter any day over a treasure hunter. At least the deer hunters shoot each other every now and then, which keeps down the loony population. Hand me that see-gar, hon."

He dumps out the last three malt balls into his hand and crumples the white bag. He looks at the two bills on the counter and scoops them up. "And they spend more'n two dollars. First sale I've made today, too."

"He did ask you for a new shovel," I remind him. I hand him the cigar; he props it on a chair arm.

"Lee," he says, "you're just too sensible for your own good. Now listen: the strong takes the weak, and the weak takes the rest."

"What?"

"Ephesians," he says.

"Ephesians what?"

"Fifty-eight sixteen."

That's a trick of Graham's. There probably isn't a fifty-eighth chapter in Ephesians, but if there is, you can bet your life it isn't what he said. "Isn't it time to go home yet?" I say. "I'm dying to see Malillie."

He looks at his watch. "Sure as hell is. Nobody else will be in this late on a day like this. You ready?"

"I just have to get my sweater. Graham, what kind of cake are we going to make for Malillie's birthday?"

"Something with a lot of chocolate," he says, cutting off lights. "Somethin' special—it isn't every day you turn seventy-five!"

Every year we collect cake recipes all winter, and exchange them by letter. Then for Malillie's birthday we make the fanciest one we've got.

"I've got a great one," I tell him. "We have to start right now soaking some cherries in brandy. It'll be an apotheosis of cakes!"

"Hey," he says. "Very impressive." He reaches for the doughnuts with one hand, his raincoat with the other. "You want a doughnut? No?"

The bell rings as we're heading out. It's Jerry Dunne, the pudgy pharmacist from across the street. He's one of my friends. What was it Daddy called him? Having not written it down, I can't for the life of me recall it. "Hi, Mr. Dunne," I say. "How have you been?" Now I can't ask Graham what that word means.

"The same," he says. "You've grown, Miss Lee."

"Indubitably," I say. Graham chuckles. I used that one all summer one year.

"I see you're still doing words-of-the-week," Jerry says.

I nod. There follows a silence. "Don't you want a doughnut?" I ask.

"No, no," he says. "I'm diabetic. So you're back already."

"Yep," I say.

"Good, good." He nods to Graham and scratches his nose. "Six okay?"

34

"You two going somewhere?" I ask.

"Out to dinner," says Graham. "That's all."

Jerry Dunne nods. "Two old bachelors, you know." The doorbell tinkles when he leaves. Graham gets the last of the lights.

"You'll miss having dinner with Daddy," I say.

He snaps his fingers. "Gee, that's right! I sure do wish I could change it, but I just can't." He clucks, and furrows his brow, and I don't let on I know it's just politeness on his part.

"Where are y'all going?"

"Ah, who knows?" he says, locking the door. "Paris, Madrid, or Roanoke, probably."

"Funny, how he said 'two old bachelors,' when he's married."

"Wife's in Charleston, with her sister," Graham says. "Now come on; let's see if we can get this Model A of mine up the hill."

4

"MALILLIE?" I CALL, SOFTLY, BECAUSE THE DARKNESS OF THE HOUSE chastens my voice as a church would. "Daddy?" No answer. Daddy loves this house, dark and antique filled. I do too. But Mama says the darkness is depressing, loves yellow and green and bright pink and new stuff. Daddy is always telling her, "There's a perfectly good bed up at Mama's we could get. You don't need to buy a new one." And she always says, "I don't want any antiques." Then he starts in about wasting money, then she goes on about how antiques depress her, and

35

he ought to let her buy new furniture. And somewhere in between they compromise: new but cheap. She hates it, and he resents spending the money.

Through the dark hall where I used to think dragons lived when I was little is Malillie's sitting room where she spends a lot of time, going up to her bedroom only at night, only sometimes. Often she sleeps on the cot in here, which always looks to me narrower than her body.

She's asleep, propped in the big chair like an overstuffed and sagging doll, snoring gently. It's lovely here, with the soft drip of rainwater from the eaves onto the shrubbery outside. The walls have a faded brown trellis design with ancient morning glories, and heavy faded blue curtains like a movie theater lobby, and bookshelves halfway up all the walls.

I hate to disturb Malillie, so I just stand and look at her for a minute, feeling love and sorrow. She's probably gone all day without eating a thing, but she never gets thin. I never knew of anybody to detest being fat so much as my grandmother. She's hungry all the time, but tries to avoid eating, tries to live on black tea. Dozens of her little china teapots are always scattered around the house. Every two or three hours she brews up a fresh pot, and part of Bessie's job is to go around with a tray collecting up Malillie's used teapots and cups and saucers from where she's abandoned them on sills, tables, even chairs. Sometimes there are a dozen from one day. And all of it to keep from eating.

Right now I can see three teapots and four cups from where I'm standing. I start to gather them up, and she wakes up with the first tiny clink. "Oh, Lee! Child!" She struggles up, holding out her arms. Hugging her, sinking in, I see up close the wispy corkscrews of angel hair on her neck, the dew in the soft folds of fat skin. She smells powdery like the linen

36

closet, like my bed and towels, like all the good summers of my life.

"Let me look at you!" she cries, who can hardly see at all. The same glandular disease that has made her fat has also caused her to be nearly blind. She pushes me away to look, gives a sigh, and seems to be trying to taste what something in her mouth is. "You're absolutely beautiful!" And she smiles in my direction. "I had no intention of napping today. I don't want to miss a second of you, not a second! Your father told me he let you off downtown."

"Where is he now?"

"Upstairs, washing up. We've been having the nicest time! Oh, darling, let's have some tea. Where's Graham?"

"He's putting the car away." I guess he will avoid Daddy as long as possible.

"Tell me how everything is," she says. "How I long to see Kate and the little boys!"

I lead the way to the kitchen, dark and still as nighttime. To the left my eye catches a quick movement on a shelf of blue canisters marked RICE, SUGAR, FLOUR, TEA, COF-FEE. A mouse. It stops at the turning of my head, stands on its hind legs, and twitches its nose in my direction. When I turn on the light, it flees back along the edge of the shelf, behind the cans. Malillie moves slowly toward the pine table in the middle of the floor.

"Just look at you," she says. "You're so grown up. A teenager!"

"I know," I say. "I'm trying not to let it show too much."

She laughs gently. "Now," she says. "Tell me all about Kate and the boys." So I do, all the while running water into the speckled blue kettle and setting it on the stove while she

37

sits slowly, heavily, at the table, listening. Her wrinkled fingers trace its markings of burns, stains, gouges, and her face is peaceful as she reads its braille message. "Maybe next summer," she says, "you can *all* come."

When I've lit the gas flame, and the water has started to purr, heating, she says, "I wonder why Graham isn't home yet."

I turn, surprised. But just as I start to say, I told you—, I remember. The stroke. "He's home," I say. "He's just gone to put his car up."

"Oh, yes," she says.

"He's going out to supper, with Mr. Dunne."

"Oh, he is?" she says. "I wonder what Mrs. Dunne is doing for dinner."

"I wondered the same thing," I say, "so I asked. She's visiting her sister in Charleston. You want me to make you a cheese sandwich?" We're both crazy about rat-cheese sandwiches on light bread, fried in butter until the cheese oozes out the sides.

"Oh, honey, not now," she sighs, adding, "not that I wouldn't love it."

"I know. Me too." I smile at her. "But there's no such thing as thin enough, right?"

"You really *are* the most sensible child! You'll be on the front seat in heaven!"

It's one of her favorite sayings, though I am not sure she even believes in heaven. She sets her teacup down with a little clink.

I roll my eyes. "I see I'm never going to hear the end of this *sensible* stuff. I'm marked forever."

"Oh, but it's absolutely true," she protests.

"It's absolutely *boring*," I say, sitting down across from her.

"I'm so proud of you, darling," she says. "Tell me about the award."

I sigh, but it's downright nice to have someone that interested in me. "Well," I begin, "let's see. Most Patriotic was one. Pat Dyne got that one. She was new this year. The first day we said the pledge to the flag, and she said it along with the rest of us. The next day she didn't say it. The third day the teacher asked her what was wrong, and she said she'd said it once, and meant it, and it seemed pointless to have to say it again. The teacher told her she'd have to leave the room if she wouldn't say it. So she left. They must have called her parents, because the second week she said it along with the rest of us, and it was like that from then on. For that she got Most Patriotic. See what I mean?"

Malillie laughs her gentle laugh. "So what were the other awards?"

"Most Helpful, Most Ambitious, Most Talented, I don't know. A few more." I stir sugar into my tea.

"Those are useful awards," she says. "I thought all they voted on these days was most popular, prettiest, cutest— although of course you'd have gotten any one of *those*, too—" She makes me feel buoyed up on pillows of pure love.

"Miss Winterbourne doesn't go in for tacky," I say.

"And who is Miss Winterbourne?"

"Adviser to the yearbook, and the typing teacher. You ought to see her. She has gray-white hair and skin, and eyes, and no makeup, and this long red scar on her forehead. Gee said one time when we saw her on the street that she had her face on upside down."

Malillie sighs. "I've been so lonesome for you! I believe I've died and gone to heaven, sitting in my own kitchen!"

"Well, I don't know about that, but you better take advan-

39

tage of having the best cheese sandwich maker in the world around."

"With you here," she mourns, "I'll *never* regain my girlish figure."

Daddy and Graham arrive from opposite directions on the scene of our tea party, and shake hands like strangers instead of brothers, though Graham tries harder. Then I think, maybe that's not fair. Graham just plain has a friendlier nature.

"Glad to see that Mother's all right," Daddy says stiffly.

"If she was any better," Graham says, winking at me, "we'd have to tie her down to keep her from going dancing every night."

"You getting along all right?" Daddy asks, in his company voice.

"Couldn't be better," Graham says. "And Lee tells me the family's been well."

Daddy goes to the cabinet and gets down a jar of tomato juice. "Lee," he says, "get me some ice." He pours some of the juice into a glass, and turns to Graham. "How's business?"

"Can't complain," Graham says. "You?" He stoops down, gets a bottle of whiskey out from under the counter, and gets down a glass. "I hope Kate and the boys are all right?"

Daddy sort of grunts. The minute I turn my back, he says, so we'll all hear, "Lee's come to help; don't either of you let her take advantage of you."

"She hasn't yet," Graham says lightly, but I can hear the wariness in his voice. "Course, it probably depends on her raising . . ." He moves toward me and the refrigerator.

"Lee's the best cook I know!" Malillie says loyally. "I just worry that you all won't be able to manage without her. I bet she's the biggest help with Green and Andrew—"

40

Of course Daddy won't bite on that. "Just don't let her get to messing up the house, making damnfool cakes and things, and running all over the county with that boy—Arland Winfrey's son—"

"His name is *Hunter*," I say, my jaws tight, my back stiff to them.

"Just keep your feet on the ground," Daddy's voice behind me says. "Where's my ice?"

"She's always just so helpful!" Malillie says desperately.

I turn around. "Just what do you mean by that?" I keep my voice low.

"Think about it," he says curtly.

But the flames are rising, and I can't control my anger. "Hunter wouldn't—" I begin hotly.

"Walks on water, does he?" Daddy asks sarcastically.

I feel helpless. My fists are clenched. Does he do this on purpose?

Graham tries to help. "Don't know about that, but I think Hunter's treading well above his knees," he says, then slaps his leg and laughs loudly.

"He's male, isn't he?" Daddy says to me. I am shaking with rage. I could kill him. "*Ice*," he says. Just like a snake. And I think, the way to get rid of the venom of a rattler is to cut off his tail, just behind his head. I take him three cubes, the exact number he wants, always, and drop them in his glass of juice. He nods, barely acknowledging. "Go set the table for supper," he says, stirring the ice cubes with his finger. "I've got to get on back tonight." Behind us, I hear Graham getting ice for his whiskey. I collect up four blue Wedgwood plates.

"I have a business dinner tonight, I'm sorry to say," Graham announces. I put one plate back—

41

—and say to myself, Please don't anyone say, *who with?* No one does.

"Oh, that's perfectly all right," Daddy says formally. Very polite, really. What was that word?

I'm glad to flee the room. I find lace mats, and silver, and water goblets, and set them out. When I come back, there's an uncomfortable silence. Daddy is staring at his tomato juice, and Malillie runs her fingers around and around her teacup rim.

So I say, "This is the first time we've ever come when it's raining, I think."

Graham leans back on the sink, takes a drink of whiskey and says, sounding relieved, "You mean you haven't *heard* about the weather?"

"No!" I say loudly. Malillie smiles and Daddy sips his juice.

"I'll tell you. First, April was hotter than a pepper sprout. Then, around May first, everything changed. Overnight. There hasn't been enough blue sky since then to make a bikini for a Playgirl of the Month. It's rained every blessed day for weeks. It's the all-time record. And storms? Been going on now for weeks. The Baptists think it's doomsday. The Methodists and Episcopalians don't know *what* to think. This preacher, Gaddis Palmer—Hy, you remember him? The one up at Hot Creek that killed his wife's lover last year, then shot himself in the foot to make it look like the guy shot him first—they haven't had the trial yet—well, he claimed—"

Suddenly Daddy's glass hits the table, splashing tomato juice up the side of it. "Graham, if they haven't had the trial, you have no right to state as fact that he killed anyone."

"Oh, hell, Hy, everyone knows it."

At this Daddy tightens his fists, and his voice is low.

42

"You have never known the truth from a hole in the ground."

Malillie looks blindly from Graham to Daddy.

I interrupt. "Wait. About the weather. And doomsday."

Graham shoots a grateful smile my way, and tips up his glass. But his face is red. "Yeah. This preacher I was—Brother Palmer? He says he looked up during a thunderstorm and saw the finger of God pointing right down at Lavesia."

"What's it supposed to mean?" I ask.

"Search me," Graham says. "Personally, I figure God meant to point at Roanoke or Lynchburg, and maybe couldn't see what with all the rain. Course, that's just my opinion," he adds, glancing at Daddy. "There's a lot more sin in those places than in Lavesia."

Daddy stares grimly at the table, saying nothing, his juice in front of him nearly gone.

"It sure seems that way to me," I agree.

Then nobody says anything, so after a second, I wade in again. "Every time it rained last year, we either went caving or to the movies," I recall.

Graham nods. "If the rain keeps up, it'll be a good summer for caving."

"You be careful, fooling around in caves," Daddy mutters. "Damnfool thing to do."

Graham glances at me, then over at Daddy. Then, with an exaggerated motion, he hauls his long arm out of his sleeve and peers at his watch. "By golly," he says, "I'm going to have to be going. I'm late as it is."

"I'll go get supper ready," I say, following him. At the door Graham mutters, too low for anyone but me to hear, "Throw a little hot fat on him. Maybe he'll leave." I act like I didn't hear.

Outside the kitchen door, Graham puts his finger to his lips, and motions me over. "Got a piece of money for you, honey." He produces the two dollars the treasure hunter gave him out of the little pocket right at his belt, and pushes it into my hand. "Listen. I want you to go to Tatum's tomorrow and order up the best chocolate soda in the house."

I try to protest. "It's everything you earned today, Graham!"

"Poo!" he whispers back. "It was raining. Nobody shops in the rain." He hushes me, insists.

So I take the money and tuck it in my loafer, grinning. Graham knows chocolate sodas are my favorite, and that there isn't another place in Virginia that makes them the right way anymore, that has a fountain, old-fashioned glasses, a marble counter, and real whipped cream instead of some tasteless polyester foam. Only in Lavesia.

Tuesday, June 6

5

THIS IS HOW I FIRST MEET MR. OAKLEY: I'M WHIRLING AROUND ON one of the high black stools at Tatum's Drugstore until it threatens to pull away from under me and sling me out the door into the rainy street. Jerry Dunne's not in. Cool, sweet, I envision my soda, topped with a mountain of snowy ice cream, whipped cream running down the glass. Daddy's gone, and Malillie and I played canasta this morning. Now Malillie and Bessie are discussing the grocery shopping, and insisted I come downtown for my soda. Perfect beginning for a perfect summer, is what I figure.

If I can just get old Sourpuss to notice me—Mrs. Bergenson.

It isn't like she has a lot of customers, just me and this old man, sort of bushy black hair with gray, in work clothes and a plaid shirt, standing over by the magazine rack. He keeps glancing out, maybe waiting for the rain to quit.

Green mirror whirls by, gray milkshake machine, upside-down glasses, chrome spouts for cherry syrup, vanilla, chocolate, cola. "I scream you scream we all scream for ice cream," I say, chanting half to myself, half to make her ask me what I want.

"You're going to make yourself sick," Mrs. Bergenson says, turning as I zoom past her hair net, green uniform, candy counter, window streaked with rain, Tatum's backward in gold.

"No, I'm not," I say. "My stomach is impervious."

"What do you want," she says tersely.

"Chocolate soda," I snap back.

I spin again, thinking about my stomach. It is lined with stainless steel; I never get sick. I never met a food I couldn't eat. Mama breaks out in hives at strawberries and tomatoes, and throws up if she drinks gin. She claims to be allergic to dog hair and dust. I suspect at least some of the allergies are in her mind, especially the ones that mean she can't clean house and we can't have a pet.

I'm glad to be able to use last week's word: *impervious*. Graham told me years ago when I started, if you use a word three times, it will belong to you forever. So every week I find a new word, then try to find three places to use it. If the soda is as good as I hope, I'll tell Graham it is the *apotheosis* of sodas: a glorified ideal. But I can't imagine where else I'm going to be able to work this one in.

"Then you'll break the stool," Mrs. Bergenson says. "So stop."

Sighing, I grab the marble counter and stop myself, shutting my eyes tight to the arcing feel of rainbow and shooting stars behind my closed lids.

When I open them, she's putting a glass down in front of me. Brown clear liquid with soapsuds on top? "What's *that?*" I ask.

"Coca-Cola," she says.

"Coca-Cola?" I repeat.

"You asked for a Coca-Cola. There. It. Is."

"Me?" I say. "Oh, no. I asked for a chocolate soda."

"Coca-Cola is what you said. That's thirty-five cents." Her chin shoves forward.

"I can't drink that," I say. "Do you know what it does to your stomach?"

Her little eyes blaze at me. "I don't know about that. But it's what you ordered, and it's what you get."

But the old man, now reading magazines, turns, and clears his throat. Mrs. Bergenson glares at him, reading without paying. "The girl said 'chocolate soda.' "

I could cheer! I nod fast at my unsuspected hero. "That's right," I say. "I definitely said *chocolate soda.*' "

She stands there, tight in the mouth as a rattlesnake. I see her deciding, eyes glittering. She looks down at the fountain glass, untouched, now with no foam on top. Then her hand strikes out and whisks it away and dramatically dumps it in the sink, leaving foam to hiss evilly in the drain.

"A grilled cheese with mayonnaise to go," the man demands, putting up the magazine. Mrs. Bergenson makes no indication she's heard. She keeps on washing dishes in her greasy dishwater, now ignoring both of us.

I perceive it is my turn to help him out. "One time," I say loudly, "my father—Hiram Eldridge, Jr.—put a piece of hamburger into a bottle of Coca-Cola—the only one we ever had in the house—and the next morning we saw that that hamburger had turned into gray mush. And it'll do the same *inevitable* thing to your stomach!" Satisfied, I sat back. Once I told the story to some of my friends when they asked me why I never drank Cokes, and they all said, "Gross!" but went right on drinking them.

The man nods and says, "Thatso," in a sentence that isn't either a statement or a question. Mrs. Bergenson only dips another plate into her gray water.

"It's true," I say.

He rubs his nose with the back of his hand, and presses his mouth into a straight line, which makes his face fierce. "You want a chocolate soda?"

"Well, yeah, but—" I glance at Mrs. Bergenson's back, and shrug.

"Let's go down to Fox's," he says.

"But—they don't have sodas," I say.

"Mebbe they do mebbe they don't," he says. They don't, but I slide into my raincoat anyway. Anything for a graceful exit.

As we get to the door, Mrs. Bergenson says, "Hansom, you ordered a grilled cheese."

"Done changed my mind, Ruby," he says, not looking at her. "Miserable old bat," he says outside the door, turning up his collar against the rain.

Anywhere else, I know, you wouldn't go anywhere with a stranger. But this one is just a farmer with a grizzled face, and Fox's is only a gas station with groceries along one wall and a freezer in the back. "This is my uncle's store," I say, as we go by.

"Funny name," he says, squinting as the raindrops bounce off his face.

"It comes from India," I tell him. "When the king gets mad at someone in India, he gives that person a white elephant. Can you imagine having to take care of it? But see, you can't refuse a gift from the king, and you can't give it away or anything, so you're stuck." I glance sideways at him, but his face is still squinting at raindrops.

When we get to Fox's I follow him around, curious about how he's going to find something that's not there. "Help y'self, Hansom," Mr. Fox says. Then, "Why, Lee Eldridge! You back already? I declare, it don't seem a week since you left. I declare you have grown!"

"How are you?" I ask.

"Wal," he says, "if I'd had any idea I was gonna live this long, I'd of killed myself a long time ago. Ha, ha!"

I keep watching the old man as I chat with Mr. Fox, who sure hasn't put in a soda fountain that I can see. In fact, if he's put in a new box of cornflakes or can of baked beans since last summer, you can't tell it.

The old man picks up a bottle of Canada Dry Soda, then a little brown can of chocolate syrup with dust thick on the top. Then he leans into the freezer, comes up with a pint of vanilla ice cream. Now I see what's going on, but where are we going to make them? He comes back toward the front. "You see any paper cups?" he asks me.

Mr. Fox looks from him to me, and back to him again. "What you doin' sneaking around here, Hansom?" he asks.

"Making sodas is all," the man replies, deadpan. "You got big paper cups?"

"What? For you?" he says to me. "You better watch out for this guy," he joshes. He reaches way up to the top shelf and gets a packet of large cups with gold flowers on them.

Handsome. I don't think it's a very apt name. "Where you keep the church keys at, Buck?" he says.

"On the wall over there, along with the egg beaters and knives and flashlights."

"Y'all know each other," I say, somehow relieved. I've known Mr. Fox for years.

My friend makes V-shape holes in the top of the can of syrup. "Run a store myself—out 889, Paradise Mountain Road," he says, a fat stream of syrup running into a cup.

"Ain't no competition a-tall," Mr. Fox calls out, shoving some cans to the end of a shelf.

"Oh, yeah," I say. "We go caving there, my uncle Graham and I."

49

"You and ever-body else," he says dryly. "Here's to you." And he hands me a cup with the right kind of foam on the top. I'm delighted. Mr. Fox shakes his head when invited to join us, but watches us with amusement.

And a while later I watch him drive off in a beat-up old black pickup carrying a bag with bread, cheese, and mayonnaise, and the rest of the soda stuff. He doesn't wave or anything. "He's an odd bird," Mr. Fox says, moving a toothpick around in his mouth.

"He seemed real nice," I say.

He looks at me thoughtfully. "Don't know as I'd get mixed up with the likes of him," he says. "He's one of them crazy treasure hunters. He s'posed to of shot at some people once. Loony. You ask your uncle about Hansom Oakley."

The rain's stopped. It still isn't time for Graham to go home. Through the store window I can see him showing a man and a woman the Queen Anne furniture, gesturing wildly in the air. I stick my head in the door, and over the tinkling bell call that I'll ride on home. He waves.

I pedal up Maple to Back Street, along Rough Creek, muddy after the rain, with jewelweed and spearmint dripping on its banks. Lavesia's so small that a few bulldozers could just appear off the interstate exit early one morning and erase the town by noon—gone without trace, the creek bank left to the animals again, the scars of the ground left to heal, the cellar holes abandoned to overgrow in honeysuckle.

Back Street leads out of town up the hill to Malillie's. I pedal hard, panting and out of shape. I'll pay with sore legs tomorrow. It's been a strange but wonderful afternoon: she, meaning Mrs. Bergenson, got what she had coming; I still have Graham's two dollars plus a chocolate soda foaming inside my stomach; plus the whole summer ahead. I pump up the hill toward home, my raincoat scratching my legs and flapping against the spokes of Graham's old bicycle at every dip in the steep road, breathing wet road and stone and cows and trees and grass, just plain glad to be back.

Sunday, June 11

6

MORNING DAWNS CLEAR, DESPITE GRAHAM'S GLOOMY PREDICTIONS
that it will rain all summer. "Who designed your outfit,
Genghis Khan? Wernher Von Braun?" Graham wants to
know, as I meet him in the kitchen. It's one of his favorite
lines. He grins and waves a spatula.

For caving, you dress in several thin layers of clothes and
waterproof shoes with good treads, since caves are slick. You
wear a waterproof jacket because caves drip. You carry a
flashlight clipped to your belt or pocket, and unless you
intend to stay where you can see daylight, you carry about a
quarter of a mile of twenty-five-pound test fishing line on a
light reel. Then when you want to go beyond the reach of
light, you tie an end to something near the entrance so you
can find your way back. So I make a face at Graham and
ignore him.

"You making pancakes?" I ask. I love Sundays, when
Graham cooks special breakfasts and doesn't have to go to
work.

He turns indignantly. "What are you, a Yankee? It's *battercakes*. You wouldn't be alive today if your ancestors had

made that mistake. During the Civil War they shot anyone around here who said *pancakes*. Proved they were Yankee infiltrators. Besides, these are crepes suzette."

"Well, they *look* like pan—uh, battercakes."

"I don't believe how parochial you are. They're a *very* famous French dish."

"What's *parochial* mean?"

"Rural. Country. Never been to the city. Here, slice up this orange as thin as you can. Paper-thin. So thin you can see through it."

Butter and vanilla scent the air. I slice the orange carefully, while Graham stirs and talks. "Lots of words like that. Anyone sneaking around here saying 'I guess it'll rain,' was liable to end up with a bullet hole to breathe through. 'I *reckon* it'll rain.' They say the same thing was true up North. A Southerner could learn a Yankee accent, say all the words right, but sooner or later he'd slip up and call an older lady ma'am and it'd give him away. You just can't help it if that's how your mama taught you."

I fix a tray with Limoges china plates and cups, a pot of tea for Malillie and coffee for us. We eat the folded little circles swimming in orange sauce at a card table by the sitting-room window. Outside sun lights from underneath the green maple leaves still drooping under the weight of last night's rain. They are translucent and jewel-like. It's the best breakfast I've ever had.

"Is Hunter going caving with you?" asks Malillie.

"No," I begin. "He—"

"—has to go to church," finishes Graham. " 'The woods a temple more worthy . . .' Wordsworth," Graham says quickly.

I roll my eyes heavenward, and Malillie says, "My son, the

53

expert on English poetry." We all laugh. I tell them Hunter is coming over tonight after supper.

"What will you do while we're gone?" I ask Malillie, when we're finished, guilty at the thought of leaving.

"Oh, goodness," she says. "I'll watch television or read, I suppose. I adore a Sunday alone."

Going out, it occurs to me she can't do either. I can only hope I'll be like her when I'm old. "I'm going to have a fried cheese sandwich for lunch," she calls behind me.

"Don't you dare!" I call back. "We're having them for supper."

To get to Paradise Mountain, you drive about six miles out and turn off on Route 664, then take 713 past fences buried under honeysuckle vine, past the country store and on to 889. If you take the left fork, you go to Montvale. The second left fork would take you to the Peaks of Otter, but you keep straight. Graham has the top down on his big old car, and the wind lifts the hair off my neck.

Suddenly, there is Oakley's store, and I remember that I've forgotten to ask Graham about Mr. Oakley. I open my mouth to but Graham says, "Some caver thinks he's found a prehistoric fireplace, with some bone fragments, inside Paradise. It was in the paper a few months back. I saved it for you; I've got it somewhere."

Paradise Cave is safe, uncluttered, with lots of crannies and ledges to explore. There's a gentle mud slide of about twenty feet, then an enormous room right there with the opening in plain sight. We've looked for passages beyond the room before, and Graham has a rope so we can scale walls. "Do you figure it was Indians?" I ask.

"Who knows? It's inhabitable, I'd think."

I lean my head happily back into the sunshine and warm wind. The road dips down to go under a stone culvert built to support the railroad that ran for less than five years before it was destroyed in the Civil War and never rebuilt. The culvert has a cement trough down one side for water to flow through that comes out and down the mountain in wet weather. We emerge just as the sun goes behind a cloud.

Route 889, on the other side of the culvert, is dirt and very narrow. You have to park in the ditch or creek to get off the road. The big gray convertible cruises half into the ditch and tilts lovingly in the direction of the creek, leaning into the matted growth of weeds and honeysuckle. The sky's white, with a distant grumble of thunder rolling up high over the mountain.

I manage to negotiate the fence without catching my clothes. Some bored holsteins graze listlessly, looking up to stare at us. Suddenly Graham looks up and says, "Did you bring lunch?" Already he's sucking his second roll of butter-rum Life Savers.

"Lunch?" I say. "We just finished breakfast."

"What's in that bag?" he wants to know.

"Just spoons and a sieve to dig with."

Graham just stands there, looking like a scarecrow. "You expect me to cave all day on an empty stomach?"

"Graham," I say. "Actually, I don't expect you to walk across the room on an empty stomach. But if you wanted food, why didn't *you* bring it?"

"For Most Sensible, you're the pits. They'd take your title away if they knew about this. Forgot lunch."

"I *didn't* forget. I didn't *plan* to bring lunch." I feel hot and irritated. "Listen," I say, "I'll race you to the top—that clump of old cedars? Whoever loses has to buy lunch. Okay?"

He looks suspicious. Then he looks at the sky. "I better put the top up," he says.

"You're scared I'll win," I say.

"Are you kidding? Me scared? Did I ever tell you about the time I unwrapped a ten-foot snake from around the water heater in the middle of winter? Or the time that drunken fool tried to hold me up at closing time?"

I turn my back. "I'm starting," I say. I bound out, through periwinkle and lacy asparagus and everything else crowding up from the spongy ground. I hear Graham's outraged holler behind me. My boots squelch with each step. Skeleton shrubs from last year tag my jeans and grab at my jacket, like the past trying to hold me back. My hair flies out behind, then falls, a light whip on my shoulder.

"No fair, Lee!" I hear Graham yell, far behind, probably still on the road side of the fence, maybe caught up in the barbed wire. Graham the Fearless. I don't turn around to see. "Wait up!" he cries. But I won't wait for his silliness.

The sun comes out briefly as I head across the low meadow for the first landmark, a huge sycamore at the tree line. I search ahead among the leaves for the next, the boulder as big as a castle embedded in the mountainside. White daisies shine like stars as I come into the dark under the trees, then the ground clears, grows rockier, a faint path zigzagging upward.

Panting, I come at last to the huge boulder, and remember the spring, a tiny oasis of wet and bright moss on the mountainside.

The climb is very steep, and I'm thirsty. Gee could probably beat me; he's light and quick as a rabbit. But I'll beat Graham easy.

I'll stop and have a drink. My feet pick the way for me, down, swinging back to the left, and then I can smell the water.

7

THE SPRING LIES UNDER THE IMMENSE BOULDER, ROCKS BEETLING above and around it, a few slender trees clustered nearby. The water, bright as ginger ale, trickles out a flat hole in the side of the hill into a shallow basin about ten feet wide, and flows on over the far lip to form one of the creeks that meanders down the mountain and through the culvert. The moss-bright rocks hanging above it appear to glow green, to gleam from behind in that deep shade. The pool's edge is tangled with watercress and ferns. I know I have a few minutes before Graham comes this way.

The water looks pure, filtered by layers of rock and soil and time, and I'm thirsty from my hard uphill sprint, so I lie on my stomach on a rock at the edge of the pool, wriggling forward until I can drink. I imagine Graham barging up the hill, and feel a pang. Still . . .

The pool bottom, a foot below, is as clear as if there is nothing between me and it. I stare down at my face, sort of narrow, quite pale, with straight brown eyebrows, and big dark-rimmed glasses. I don't dislike my face exactly, but it hasn't got much character. Malillie's face has character. My hair, brown and straight, is clasped behind with a barrette, and I watch as it slides over my shoulder and barely touches the water, *plp*. The surface ripples, then calms again. Framing my face is the dark cress with tiny white flowers that quiver slightly in the invisible air. I pick a piece and chew it, know-ing that it will burn my tongue. It's hot after it flowers in May. Then I look past my face at rocks, dead leaves, a bottle half-buried in silt, a fern suspended in the water, blackish specks . . .

"Lee!" Graham's voice reaches uphill, closer than I thought, and I startle. Water splashes up on my glasses. "Wait up!" he calls.

"Oh, sh—oe polish! Now he'll win," I whisper to my image, "and I'll have to buy lunch!" I snatch off my glasses to clean them quickly.

At that precise moment, I lift my head and find myself staring directly into the small hole where the water comes out of the mountainside. A sly trick comes to mind. Can I answer Graham? draw him this way? then crawl through the hole and hide? then, when he comes looking, burst out and get a head start the rest of the way?

I'd get dirty . . .

It will be a tight squeeze, maybe even impossible . . .

I can get into places no one else can. I'm long, but I'm also skinny . . . and it would serve him right.

Suddenly to my left is a movement. I jerk my head toward it: only light and shadow, white and dark, are there. I keep staring, sure I've seen *something*. With no glasses, I'm at a disadvantage. Did something move back into the camouflaging trees, leaving the leaves atremble? I put my glasses back on, but the sharper edges make deeper seeing more difficult. Yet in the corner of my eye, or mind, was the impression of a—man. Not Graham, somehow, that I'm sure. Besides, *his* voice came from the right.

"Lee?" Graham's voice is accompanied by the crunching of underbrush close by.

A flat, moss-covered rock lies in the creek bed just below the cave's mouth. It rises out of the water a few inches.

One leap puts me on it, balancing precariously, my arms stuck out at my sides making like a seesaw. The entrance is even smaller than I thought from several yards back, though it opens out a little beneath the overhang. I'll get wet knees, since I'll have to climb in through the stream bed, and muddy from top to bottom.

I hesitate. Then his voice comes again, only a few yards away. I am about to be caught! "Cheaters never prosper—remember that, Lee Eldridge!"

I grin to myself. It's like playing hide-and-seek again. What difference if I get muddy? Mama's not here to fuss. I measure the hole with my eye, then call, "Oh, Graham! Here I am, just having a little drink over here at the spring!"

He's coming, the rustling and snaps of his footsteps clearer. "You jerk," he calls, sounding out of breath. I glance up at the white sky above the trees, adjust my glasses, put up one knee, grab a reliable-looking root, and tug at it. It holds.

In a second I'm kneeling in icy water, skin drawing back from the cold as it spreads, peering into blackness and feeling for dry land. I find it to my left, scramble up on a ledge just above water level, and pull my legs in behind me. Roots or ferns tickle my face, and, tightening myself against the impulse to scream and back out, I reach up and out tentatively.

Not much overhead space; my arm encounters dirt, which sends a dry shower down in front of my face, then more roots or rock, impossible to tell which.

Behind me, light enters the cave, but I am surely hidden from an outsider's view. I feel ahead and to my left, stretching my arm up and out. The ground stays level, and the cave seems to open up into the mountain. I inch forward on my knees, feeling each space first with my hands. When you can't see, someone told me once, other faculties take over, grow stronger. I pull myself to a sitting position. The trickle of water out of the cave has a slight sound-reflection indicating a room at any rate large enough to echo.

Gradually I can see: it is not totally black. My eyes catch a

59

fuzzy shaft of light coming from some opening high above, probably at the bottom of a sinkhole. The stream, glistening softly, veers off to the right. Crouching, I inch back a little farther, then fumble for my flashlight. I turn it on and play it upward, over rocks, dark murky shapes that could be stalactites or roots, earth.

Where I am is a rough-smooth widening bank, steep side going inward as it rises like the inside of a beehive or vault. Huge rocks are hanging over my head, an upside-down landscape that looks ready to crash.

I only want to see how far I can go. The entrance is still at my back, and I won't go any farther than I can see. The ledge takes me to the big boulder, then gives way to nothing, with the stream below. About four feet beyond, too far to jump, a possible path begins and veers sharply upward before widening out again, right beneath the single shaft of light from above. I click off my light, and the sun ray hangs like a fuzzy sword in the gloom. On again.

I move the beam up the wall, then along the floor of that higher room, about at eye level, to a clump of very big, roundish rocks, some of them half-buried in fallen dirt. But no—not a rock—that is—what? Too round for a rock, somehow. The shadows swing crazily with the slightest movement of the flashlight.

It seems to be a huge pot, for a handle is lying against the round side, maybe soldered against it with rust. I've seen pots like it in country people's yards, I think, and in antique stores. Rocks are famous for looking like other things. But I see a top is in place, under some fallen dirt. It is crammed into the narrow space between floor and wall-ceiling.

Slowly, not wanting to, really, but more like having to, I move the light again, and it lands on—a round rock, this time, surely. No. Another pot. Then another. Following the flashlight's view, I count at least eight big pots, like witches' cauldrons, lined up against the wall, sunk into the floor, dirt and rocks fallen around them.

Now I can't cut off the light, for what kind of craziness is this? As far as I can tell, they are all alike, half-out of mud and dirt. It chills my skin.

Ali Baba and the Forty Thieves. Hansel and Gretel. My mind stumbles around in old storybooks. I keep my light trained on the haphazard group, kind of trying to fend them off, whatever they are, with my beam, as I might a stunned animal. I don't turn off the light, but begin inching back toward the opening. Each cauldron looks big enough to hold—horrors!—a body! Bluebeard! I think I remember from *National Geographics* that some people one time got buried in pots. Where? When?

Indians! I've stumbled on an Indian burial. Graham said someone thought—

What else would a bunch of iron pots be doing here? I think maybe someone lived here. Just for an instant, I am terrified anew: a bear family, food stored in those pots, could tear me to pieces: both ravenous beasts and humanized creatures out of books. They are slavering and wild, yet dressed in red overalls, reasonable and cuddly and human.

I back up farther. Nothing could entice me to turn my back on them. I have to get out.

"Leeeee!" Good old Graham: His voice curls in over the sound of trickling water. My foot slips, and the flashlight crashes from my hand down between some rocks, a good yard out of reach. It trains one clear circle of light upward onto a smooth rock as the echo of the clatter fades.

I freeze, unable to move, and Graham calls me a second

61

time, then, with growing force, a third. I want to answer, but I'm afraid any sound I make might awake—what? Are they creeping toward me? What can I do? My eyes *hurt* from trying to stare into that dark.

Finally I take a deep breath, back up feeling for light, and finally dare to dart a look over my shoulder to make sure of the entrance. I cannot believe how small it is, and for an instant I *know* I can't fit. "Graham!" It comes out in a hoarse half-whisper, like a moment in a dream when you try to yell and your voice won't work.

Then I force down my panic: I got in. Of course I can get out.

Can't I?

Barely. Sliding on my back, scraping my stomach, I feel with my feet for the rock under the opening. Then I make the leap onto solid, mushy ground even before the water, painfully cold, has soaked through my clothes onto my back.

I blink at the rush of light, this white morning, and a long way off, thunder grumbles. I am alive, alone, my knees so weak I'm not sure I can walk. I try to breathe calmly, but that mechanism isn't working right, and my heart pounds.

"Graham?" I say. No answer. No wonder. My voice sounds weak and strange. I clear my throat and try again. "Graham!" I stand still to listen. Then, as fast as I can, getting stronger as I go, I sprint my way up the hill to the cedar grove, and start again to call Graham.

First only the wind replies, huffing up a storm. I can smell rain coming. I can't decide what to do. Then, Graham's voice floats upward, a cry from another world. Heavy clouds gather overhead.

I meet him coming up the mountain, sweating profusely. "What the hell happened to you?" He's mopping his head with a balled-up handkerchief.

I open my mouth to explain, but it's all so silly—the fear, the feeling of being in a fairy tale—and a warning, a red flag, goes up in my mind: Graham won't keep a secret. "I—got lost. I was getting a drink, and slipped in the creek. I couldn't find the cedar grove. I went back to look for you—"

I indicate my muddy clinging jeans as proof, but find I cannot meet his eyes.

"They shoot bird dogs that lose their way," he says. "I don't see how the hell you—"

Pots? Eight at least. Eight huge, old-fashioned rusty iron pots with tops. Maybe more. Did the Indians have iron pots? I comb through what facts I can remember from school, wishing I'd paid more attention. Clay, I remember that. Clay in big coils, wound like snakes, then smoothed down to make the sides of a pot. But iron?

Treasure? The Beale Treasure? Of course not; it doesn't exist, one; and two, it's four *tons* of gold and silver. I figure that must be enough to fill a whole room. Then what? I can't concentrate. I want to tell Graham, to get him to go back in there with me. But he fusses on, blaming me for making him forget to put up the top, for forgetting lunch, for getting lost.

None of it makes sense. A raindrop hits my nose then, and then one hits Graham's forehead, and we suddenly are running for the car instead of the cave. The cows stand bunched, staring gravely at us, in the meadow at the bottom of the mountain.

For some reason I'm crying. Graham notices, stops. "Honey!" he says. "You're not upset about lunch? I was only teasing—"

I snuffle a little, and he gives me a Kleenex, and we get the top up before the car's too wet.

"Tell you what," Graham says. "Since lunch is your

63

responsibility, the way I see it, why don't we have cheese sandwiches and save the chicken for supper, and you can invite Hunter to come early?" He puts his arm around my shoulder and gives me a little hug. How can I not hug him back? Rain splatters the windshield, and he turns on the wipers. "Honey, punch in the lighter and peel this here cigar," he says.

All the way home we're just ahead of the storm.

8

THE BIG OLD HALL CLOCK STRIKES TEN TIMES. MALILLIE STANDS BY MY door in her white nightdress, casting a shapeless shadow by the dim hall light. I don't understand myself. Why didn't I tell someone what I thought I saw? I guess I just figured it would get taken away from me if I told someone—at least if I told someone grown up. I tell myself I mustn't upset Malillie. I wanted to talk to Hunter, but I never got to see him alone. Now it will be days and days until I see him again.

In the hall, Malillie says her good-night verse the way she has all my life: "Good night, sleep tight, wake up bright in the morning light, And do what's right with all your might. Good night. . . ."

And I don't know what's right. I don't know. Years ago, it seems, Malillie at lunch said: "How was the caving, darling?"

Graham saved me by leaping right in. "Caving!" he echoed. "Lee got lost, so we never—"

"Lost?" Malillie said. "You didn't tell me—"

"Oh, it wasn't anything," I said. "How lost could you get on Paradise Mountain? Boy, don't these sandwiches look yummy?"

"Honey, I don't understand," Malillie said gently. "I thought you *couldn't* lose yourself caving. Graham, dear, you *know* you've promised me you wouldn't go in a cave that wasn't perfectly—"

"Malillie, it wasn't Graham's fault." Then I remembered my story. "I wasn't in a cave," I said, realizing I had just lied to my grandmother. I'll tell her later, I promised myself. She'd never take anything away from me, and I'd tell her very calmly, and she wouldn't tell. I swallowed and went on. "We were just—racing up the mountain and I lost the way and got turned around—" I looked over at her quickly, to see if she believed me, trying to remember if that was the way I'd told it to Graham.

"Poor thing doesn't know the difference between *up* the mountain and *down* the mountain," Graham said to Malillie in a loud whisper, handing me my plate.

I took a bite of my sandwich, and it was like sawdust. But the subject wouldn't go away. In the morning paper, Graham had found an article about the Natural Bridge Cavern he thought we'd like. It is always my job to read such articles aloud, since Malillie can't see to read them herself.

The Natural Bridge Cavern was explored more than a hundred years ago, but abandoned when the men began to hear ghostlike moans coming closer and louder, like wailing. I glanced at Malillie; her eyes were closed and her face perfectly placid, as she slowly chewed a bite of her cheese sandwich. I went on. The diggers decided it must be the sound of Indians buried there long ago, so they left fast, leaving tools and a ladder deep in the cavern.

I shivered, and forced down another mouthful, as Graham poured us tea. "Go on," Malillie said, so I knew she wasn't asleep.

Today the assumption was (I read) that it must have been air whistling through crevices, or perhaps a trapped bobcat howling. They've put a track through it now, and you can ride through in a little train.

Oh, what was abandoned in my cave? What have I found? Other people find stuff: everything from four-leaf clovers to Civil War buttons and cannon shot. Graham found a ten-dollar bill last summer flapping around in the gutter. Once Mama found a gold watch in a taxi and wore it for a long time until it broke. Everyone but me finds arrowheads in the mountains, proving that Indians hunted here long ago. Mr. Fox has a landscapelike picture in the store constructed of 245 of them that he and his family found.

But I never find things. I can't think of one thing I've ever found. Malillie said, "This sounds wonderful. I've just been waiting for a cave with a train, so I can see what it is *you* see in caves. We'll have to go soon."

"It's hard to see anything much," I said. And for a minute I felt better. It was probably just a mistake, an illusion, or just a bunch of old rusty pots someone put there, then forgot.

But suddenly Malillie, still standing outside my door, interrupts my thoughts, her voice tentative in the dark. "Darling, are you all right? You seem—melancholy—today." Her voice drifts off, waiting.

"Oh, Malillie," I say, guilty at having forgotten her, standing there in the drafty hall, "I'm fine. Really. Please go to bed."

"All right, honey." Her shape, blurred without my glasses, moves heavily away. Her good-night verse still echoes: *Do what's right. . . ?*

What's right? What's right? Shall I go back? Maybe open a pot, see what's in it? What would Daddy do? Thunder answers, a long low roll that seems to travel a long way through the mountains.

I turn over, but I won't sleep. I have to think about Hunter. When he arrived today, *something* was different. At once I thought of Barbara and Suzanne and Camille calling him my boyfriend, and felt my face get hot. He saw it, too, and then *his* face got red. "Hi," I said, and "Hi," he said, at the same moment. I didn't know what to do then, and couldn't remember how we'd done this in the past. I guess it didn't matter. "You look wonderful," I said then. It sounded very fake.

He shifted around a little and cleared his throat and said, "The light must be bad in here." Then he swallowed, his Adam's apple swelling in his neck. "Glad you're—back," he said, only a faint imitation of his former cheerful, cheeky self.

"Oh, I always come back," I said, feeling somehow dumb.

"Aren't you early this year? Usually you don't come until Miss Lillie's birthday." And it pleased me that he had noticed, though it made my face get hot all over again. I didn't ever realize he was aware of when I came or went.

"They just couldn't stand me any longer down there in Norfolk. So Graham and Malillie said they'd take me in."

And all the time, I was trying to remember what it had been like before, and why it was different now.

When winter comes, we never write. My friends at home know about Hunter, and it's been convenient to accept their label, that he is my *boyfriend*. It was their idea, not mine. At least it wasn't my idea until they started in about it. It makes me vaguely uncomfortable, because it's kind of like they've given me something I don't deserve, something I didn't have to work for. For some reason I never could figure out, they all think it's really classy to have a boyfriend who lives somewhere else. But it makes me squirm to think about Hunter ever learning about *that*.

The first time I ever saw Hunter, he was much bigger than I was, and he had a very realistic stuffed bear on wheels that I loved. It was almost as big as I was then. He had a springhouse in his yard that made a wonderful playhouse. I played that the bear was our child, that he was the father, and I the mother, and I made lemonade in the springhouse that day with lots and lots of sugar in it, and we drank it and got very sticky, and he was nicer than any of the boys who lived near us at home, who wouldn't play house at all, but seemed bent on breaking up all my doll china. When Malillie and Mrs. Winfrey came to find us that day, I asked if I could take the bear home with me. Hunter said I could, but Malillie wouldn't let me. The next day Hunter and his mother came to Malillie's birthday party, and brought her a jar of pink soaps shaped like roses, and brought me the bear. We had pink hats and curled-up whistles, and a cake that was orange-flavored with thick white icing. Graham played the banjo for us, and we all sang "Happy Birthday," and "Row Row Row Your Boat," then Graham took Hunter and me out back when it was getting dark and set off sparklers for us. And all the time, I pulled the bear along, loving it. Hunter's Bear, I called it, and it must still be somewhere up in the attic. It was in my room for years. I ought to go look for it. We've been friends ever since then, and he still always comes to Malillie's birthday party. The year he had chicken pox, we even put the party off a week so he could come.

So what was different today? I think that every other summer, soon after I came, he showed up on his bike, just appeared, acting like it was only last week he was here. He was always cheerful, always sunburned, and fun to be with, but just a part of the landscape, as far as I was concerned. We've fished for crawdads, swum in Rough Creek, painted his porch and our kitchen one summer. We've made popcorn and ice cream and lemonade and cookies. We've ridden our bikes all the way to the Dari-Queen out on the highway. Twice he's taken me on Baptist hayrides, and one time with his church group to Lakeside Amusement Park in a hot schoolbus. I think what I like best about him is how he listens. The boys I know in Norfolk don't listen to girls at all. It's almost a matter of principle. But Hunter acts like he's never heard that you're supposed to make fun of girls, and he listens to me the way you'd *want* other people to listen—with his whole body and his whole face, and no trace of sarcasm. It's the way I want Daddy to listen.

So what's the problem? For one thing, he's taller since last summer, and really very good-looking. I'm so tall I've been taller than him now for a couple years but I think he's caught up now. I snuck looks at him during supper, hoping my yellow sundress and still-damp hair looked okay. I was aware of an awkwardness in the conversation throughout supper. Finally by dessert I was able to work it around to the subject on my mind. "Do any of you know," I asked, "did the Indians that lived around here have iron pots?"

All of them looked at me. "Iron pots?" Malillie repeated.

"You mean like cooking pots?" asked Hunter, staring at me. Thunder grumbled, a long way off.

"Well . . . yes . . ." I said.

Graham said, "I don't believe they mined iron around here until just before the war."

"You mean the Civil War?"

69

Graham made a face at me. "I don't know of any other war that's been fought around here."

Then Malillie commented about the ice cream, and Graham had to tell a story: "It's buttered almond crunch," he said. "Buck Fox got it by mistake and had it on sale. You know he won't carry anything but chocolate, strawberry, and vanilla. He says people around here like those kinds. I asked him how the hell did he know, since it was all he ever had. 'Well, they buy it, don't they?' he told me. Said this buttered almond crunch was moving real slow. I said it was because nobody knew he *had* it!"

We all laughed and everyone had seconds. Then I said, "I wonder what they cooked in."

"Who?" asked Graham.

"She means the Indians," Hunter said.

"You still worried about them?" Graham asked.

"They must have had iron after the white men came," Hunter said. "Or at least known about it."

"What did they eat, anyway?" Graham asked. "Besides deer, I mean. I'll bet they were bored as hell with deer after a while. Deer Stroganoff, deer burgers, deer pâté, deer-loaf—"

"Maple syrup," Hunter said. "I understand they knew how to make that." More thunder. I *understand. . . . ?* He sounded so—stiff!

"Wonderful!" Graham said. "Let's see: they must have had maple deer ragout, deer with maple gravy—"

"He didn't say they ate it *with* the deer," I said, suddenly feeling that Graham was making fun of Hunter.

"He didn't say they didn't, either," Graham said, winking at me.

Malillie sighed. "Well, I feel sorry for the Indians if they didn't have buttered-whatever-this-is ice cream." The sky lit up with lightning. Thunder answered it, nearer.

Hunter just smiled at me. "If this rain keeps up," Malillie continued, "we'll have a humdinger of a flood. The one in '39 I never will forget."

"I'll bet," Hunter said, looking at me, "the Indians cooked in clay pots." That's what I mean: It was like he *knew* I wanted to be back on the subject, and he was helping me. And that takes real listening. I smiled at him gratefully. Maybe things hadn't really changed so much after all. I was feeling happier.

Malillie wiped her mouth delicately. "I dearly hope we don't have a flood. But I'm glad we don't live in tornado country. I'd rather a flood any day than a tornado."

Hunter and I exchanged amused smiles.

"Bet they didn't eat any breakfast at all," Graham said suddenly.

"Why?" Hunter and I asked in unison.

Graham grinned. "Did *you* ever try to fry an egg in a clay pot?"

"Goodness!" said Malillie. "I'm having trouble following the conversation today."

"It's no wonder, Miss Lillie," Hunter said, rolling his eyes.

I decided to give it one more try. "I don't suppose—do any of you know how the Indians—the ones around here—buried dead bodies?"

"God, I didn't know teenage girls were so morbid," Graham said. "What do you want to know that for?"

"Well, I mean—did they ever bury them in pots?"

"I don't know, but probably not in their *cooking* pots," Graham said. He pushed away from the table. "Just don't

71

be putting me in the turkey roaster when I'm gone, you hear?"

"My mama says she's gonna put Daddy on the compost heap when he dies," Hunter said.

I made a shocked sort of noise, but Malillie laughed. "That sounds sensible to me!"

Graham said he had to go down to the store awhile to work on Harold's stove, so that gave me something, a funny story, to tell Hunter and Malillie. They both laughed, but Malillie said, "You know, there's a wonderful lesson there! You ought not to keep useless things. They should throw that old stove out if it's no good anymore."

Then, with Graham gone, we were awkward again. "Malillie," I said, "let me make you a fresh pot of tea." But she shook her head, and said there was a radio program she liked to listen to on Sunday nights.

So we all stood up at the same time, Hunter saying, "Miss Lillie, let me bring by some greens tomorrow," and I realized how disappointed I was when Hunter said he'd better go, as Monday would be here too soon to suit him. But as he left, he asked me to a cakewalk next Friday at his church.

I washed the dishes and then went to help Malillie up the stairs. Seeing how weary, how heavy, she seemed, I knew I couldn't tell her—at any rate, not tonight—about what I found. I promised myself that I'd tell Hunter all about it, that by Friday I'd know more . . . and that was an hour ago.

But now I am freezing and burning up at the same instant. I sit up in bed and say aloud, "The Beale Treasure!" reaching automatically for my glasses, breathing my voice into the empty dark room. I had forgotten something earlier when I thought it couldn't be. Now I am stunned. The Beale Treasure! Of course! *Everyone* knows it was buried in big iron pots.

How could I have forgotten? *That's* what was familiar, what's been eluding me all day! Iron pots! Right. Maybe nine. More than 150 years, people have been looking, and I found it!

Or did I? Just as suddenly, it seems too easy, like opening one of those game cards at McDonald's and winning ten thousand dollars.

The Beale Treasure? I have a splendid vision of all the things we can fix in this house, the cracked window panes and peeling paint. Most of the rugs are gone—sold, Daddy says, to heat the house in winter. Even when it's cold out and the furnace roars, you can feel breezes around the doors and windows. We'll get new rugs! Some of the worst places where the plaster is rotted, you can see through all the way to the outside. We'll get new everything! I know the store doesn't pay enough to keep things up; Daddy rants about that every time Graham goes to New York or Atlanta for the weekend. Once last summer while I was asleep, a big hunk of plaster fell on my bed and woke me up. I thought we should at least try to fix it, but Graham, unconcerned, just moved the bed next morning before he went to work. Still, a year later, it's not fixed. A sports car—Graham has always wanted a snazzy sports car.

Then I think of all the things we need at home: new clothes, new furniture, maybe a housekeeper to help Mama, a boat for Daddy. I can see it like heaven in front of me, a new happy life for all of us. A ten-speed bike for Gee, one of those jazzy banana bikes for Drew! And for me? I can't really think of a thing I need. Well—maybe that silver fox topper I saw once last winter in Thalhimer's window, as long as the sky is the limit.

The Beale Treasure! I hug my knees in the dark and shiver.

The Beale Treasure! Gee and Drew will absolutely *die!* I feel like getting out of bed and calling them now, this very minute. Only of course I won't.

Now. What *will* I do?

Outside, like a record beginning over again, the rain starts up. Damp air blows through the room, and the tempo of the rain hesitates, then starts again harder.

Well, Daddy, will you finally be proud of me?

I certainly can't see that it could hurt a thing to just go have another look, as soon as I can, just to see if I'm right.

9

IF SOMEONE ASKED, YOU'D HAVE TO SAY THAT LAVESIA IS AN undramatic place: for instance, the flood in 1939 that killed fourteen people is the only really severe one ever recorded—there's never been an earthquake, or a tornado. The deepest snow they ever had was about sixty years ago, thirty-six inches, Malillie says. The second deepest, in 1963, was a measly nineteen inches. It's not wild enough for bears or panthers or big rattlesnakes. The mountains are old and full of caves, and I don't think they were much, say, compared to the Rockies or Himalayas, even in their heyday.

The only murders are by jealous husbands or wives, and Graham usually says they deserved it. And Malillie is likely to reply, "Now, Graham, you'll never get to heaven on someone else's sins." In Lavesia nobody even locks their cars or houses.

There's the drive-in four miles away for entertainment, and

the Dari-Queen. In April during Garden Week buses of blue-haired old ladies from Lynchburg and Roanoke came to tour the few elegant old houses, including Malillie's, up to a few years ago. Once a man came in the store and told us he was hunting ginseng and selling it to China for forty-five dollars a pound. Graham said he had to be lying.

In fact, the *only* thing that Lavesia is famous for is that it's near the Beale Treasure. Everyone knows about it. It's like Natural Bridge, or Robert E. Lee; you couldn't be from here and not know about it. People come with boots and back-packs and shovels and Geiger counters and metal detectors and lunch boxes, and spend the weekends digging.

The story is that in January of 1822, a man named Thomas Jefferson Beale came to Morriss's Inn, somewhere near Lavesia, and put up there as a simple traveler. He stayed three months, and charmed all the ladies, and Morriss recalled him later as "a fine gentleman."

When he departed, he gave the innkeeper a tin box with the instruction to open it in ten years if he did not come back for it.

It was 1845 before Mr. Morriss remembered to open the box, which contained a letter to him, and three brittle yellowed papers filled with numbers, and numbered 1, 2, and 3.

The letter revealed that Beale had deposited a treasure underground near Morriss's Tavern. The way the letter told it, he had left Lynchburg in April of 1817 to go west to hunt for gold. After arriving in St. Louis, he and his men, thirty of them, drew up rules for living, hired a guide and three servants, and again set out to find gold on May 19, 1817.

On December 1, they arrived in Santa Fe, New Mexico, where they waited out the winter. In early March of 1818, north of Santa Fe, they followed a herd of buffalo one day up a narrow path into a hidden valley in the mountains where they found, and mined, unbelievable amounts of gold and silver. Twice some of them returned to Virginia to deposit treasure secretly.

The letter explained that paper number 1 told the exact location of the treasure, that number 2 described its contents, and that number 3 gave the names and addresses of the treasure owners. The key to these codes, the letter explained, was left with someone in St. Louis who would be getting in touch with Mr. Morriss. That person never had, never did. And then the inn, sometime after, burned down.

Code number 2, based on the Declaration of Independence, as it turned out, was soon broken, but codes number 1 and number 3 never have been.

Code number 2 revealed that the deposits were 1014 pounds of gold and 3812 pounds of silver the first time, and 1907 pounds of gold and 1288 pounds of silver the second time, plus roughly $30,000 worth of jewels, which they got in trade for gold and silver in St. Louis while coming back the second time. It further described that the entire treasure is in iron pots with iron covers, in a stone-lined vault about six feet underground.

In 1885 Morriss gave up trying to decipher the other codes, and gave the box to another innkeeper, Mr. J. B. Ward, of Lynchburg. Mr. Ward published and distributed a pamphlet with the codes, in the hope that someone would be able to decipher them. They have intrigued treasure hunters ever since, and brought them to try their luck in the mountains all around here.

There are two opinions about this thing: that the story is true, and that it's all just a hoax.

In favor of the hoax, there is no trace anywhere along the route he claims they traveled of a Thomas Jefferson Beale. And it was a big group of men. No proof of the expedition has ever been found in St. Louis or in Santa Fe. In fact, there is no trace of Beale beyond the metal box.

It seems nearly unbelievable that thirty men would agree to having their hard-won riches buried in a place secret even to them, and even more unbelievable that it could have been possible to transport four tons of precious stuff two thousand miles secretly. It has been estimated that the treasure would have made burdens for eighty to one hundred pack animals. And where did he get those nine pots without arousing suspicion?

A further puzzlement: Mr. Beale must have known he wouldn't be around to see all those people making fools of themselves. What could he have had to gain by taking all that time and energy to create a hoax so clever that the smartest people and the best computers still didn't know today if the first and third codes were even real or not?

For myself, despite the story, and all the weekend treasure hunters who'd been coming to Lavesia as long as I had, tromping all over the place, I think I, like Graham, never really believed in it. I guess that's why I got elected Most Sensible—I am not the type to get carried away with stories like that. In fact, Suzanne Jennings and I made nearly twenty dollars once by spending the night in a supposedly haunted room at her grandmother's, when Camille and Barbara and Eloise bet us money we wouldn't. Suzanne persuaded her grandmother to let her have a slumber party; the other three slept downstairs in her room, but Suzanne and I snuck up to the tower room at midnight and spent the night peacefully on Great-Grandmother Cecilia's four-poster. Of course nothing happened, except that we were late for breakfast from sleeping later than the others downstairs, and had to sneak past a cleaning woman running a vacuum cleaner to get back down to where we were supposed to be spending the night.

Friday, June 16

10

I HAVE TO GO BACK, OF COURSE, TO SEE IF I AM RIGHT, IF I CAN SEE them again. I have half-decided they'll turn out to be just round rocks after all.

Normally, the time would have gone fast, playing cards with Malillie, cooking things we love, talking and reading, just going through drawers to see what's in them. Every day I've turned the cherries in brandy that are soaking for her birthday cake, something called Black Forest Torte. I've written to Gee and Drew, printing so Gee can read it aloud. I told them about the soda, and the broken stove, and about going caving. Of course I couldn't say anything about what I found. Tonight Hunter is taking me to the cakewalk over in Clark's Grove. His older brother will drive us, even though Hunter's been driving since he was ten.

But the time has gone slower than the seven-year itch. I've kept those pots—if that's what they really are—in my head. With each day that has passed, I've trusted my memory and eyesight less. Finally, today, it's cleared off enough to get out there again.

Graham's old black bike, held together by chewing gum

and prayer, he says, does fine, sliding around a little in the churned-up mud of 889. Parking it, I worry some about whether it will be okay propped bridgelike across the swollen little creek. The sky is thick and gray, probably just waiting to start up again. My hands are trembly with excitement, and I wish Hunter were along, but he's fence mending this week in addition to his usual chores.

The greenery is higher and thicker already, threatening to overtake the world entirely after almost a week of steady rain. I nod to the sad cows as I pass. My jeans are soaked halfway up by the time I tear my way through the honeysuckle to get to the spring.

I snake through the opening again, and hear the lime-laden water echo in the cave, trickling out at the mouth, dripping softly onto the cave floor. I love the stony underground smell. I am determined to be calm this time, but I kind of wish Gee were along. Or Hunter. Or even Graham.

Getting around the big rock is difficult. Shining my light down (Malillie's, actually), I think I can see my dropped flashlight in the water. Twice my feet slip. I figure the pots must have been placed from above, instead of through the spring opening. In fact, the light hole is so high above I wonder if the pots didn't fall through a thin floor to a lower level of the cave a long time ago. My light beam shows the pots the same as before. I blink but still cannot see them clearly. Above them is a sort of hint of cloudy light today instead of the blade of sunlight. Whatever opening there is above is invisible from where I am.

Suddenly something whizzes by my head. I recoil, flinging up my arms to protect my head. A bat. They see without seeing, know those rough round shapes by heart, and want to know what I am doing here.

I feel for a fingerhold up high, my heart beating fast. I

80

think, even if I slip I can break the fall. The creek can't be very deep. Finally, straddling the rock, clinging to nearly non-existent bulges, I haul myself up to the higher level, two yards from the nearest pot.

My breathing won't do right. I have to sit and rest a minute. Putting out my lower lip, I blow the hair out of my face. Around me the air is cold. I take off my glasses and clean them before putting them on again.

I have to force my hand to touch the side of the pot.

It is cold, icy-cold, colder than the cave air, colder than time. But it is definitely real. I see myself telling Hunter tonight. There is a normal world out there.

So I will myself to be calm, and look around with Malillie's flashlight.

The third pot seems to be the one I can most easily get at without disturbing things too much. I brush off some of the loose dirt, but much more is encrusted, as hard as rock. The surface of the metal is bubbled in places, as if acid had corroded it. Another bat whizzes by, but now that I know what it is I am not frightened. Also, that one doesn't come as close as the other.

Gently, my heart beating hard, I begin to pull at the top. It won't budge. How stupid, I think, to forget to bring something to pry with. I push at it some, but it is tight, sealed by rust and lime deposits.

Do I have anything that will open it? No. I squat by the pots the same color as earth and rock and root, push my glasses up on my nose, angry at myself, wiping dirt off my hands onto my jeans, still trying to breathe normally.

But now at least I know they are boulder-shape pots, not pot-shape boulders. And another thing I know is that I have to find out what is in them.

My finger begins to hurt, and I stick it in my mouth. It

tastes bloody, or silvery. I have no idea when I cut it. I sit down on the cold cave floor beside the pots. How could I have been so dumb as to think I'd just be able to lift the tops off, as if they were so many casseroles of baked beans?

The possibility crosses my mind that I am not *supposed* to be able to open them, that I don't know the magic word that will make the tops lift off and set down gently by themselves. Then I tell myself I've been reading too many ghost stories.

Maybe they are guarded by ghosts. I sit in the dark and suck on my sore finger for a while, and think about Gee and Drew, how they would love this. They are always playing "treasure games." I can't tell what Daddy's reaction would be: maybe admiration that I found what nobody else could but more likely, annoyance: for haven't I neglected Malillie to be here at all?

After a while I go to work on the third top with one of my boots. I look around for a stone large enough to bang with, and find one, but I don't like the way the banging echoes in my ears. Also, I don't know how far the noise carries.

I try other tops, pushing and kicking, but they are worse than the first, and the last ones are wedged up under the ledge and so buried in fallen dirt that it would probably take dynamite to get them out. By then my hands are aching and raw and cold, especially the finger I cut, and the cold of the cave is beginning to seep all the way down through my nylon jacket and sweater and shirt to my skin.

At least now I know they are pots, and that there are not eight, but nine of them. I've more or less decided I'll have to tell Malillie, but I'll do it calmly, casually, even, and ask her not to mention it to Graham. "Oh, Malillie, I think I might have found the Beale Treasure. . . ."

I have a headache beginning when I leave, so I decide to stop at Mr. Oakley's store, get something to eat. Graham's theory is that all headaches are caused by low blood sugar. He told me once that was why he eats all the time, to avoid headaches. Suddenly I see Drew's five o'clock face, and hope he is happy, and miss him. It's cold and wet for June, and I am chilled to the marrow.

The store is old and dark, with a wood stove in back whose heat doesn't reach anywhere near the front. At first Mr. Oakley doesn't seem to recognize me, but I say who I am. "Oh," he says, "all out of sody-water today."

"Oh, that's okay," I say. "I think I'd like chocolate milk and Nabs today anyway."

"You out this way all alone?" he asks.

"It's only half an hour or so on my bike," I say. I pay him and put the change in my pocket and sip the chocolate milk. I walk back to the stove, and hold out my aching hands for some warmth. Looking down, I see an old plaid blanket and some kittens, three of them, curled up asleep on it, under the stove. Stooping down, I pick one up, and hold the sleepy milk-smelling ball of silvery fur to my face. It begins to purr at once. "Oh, Treasure," I murmur.

"You want a kitten?" calls Mr. Oakley. He is taking cans of tomatoes out of a box and putting them on a shelf in the back.

"Oh, I couldn't—" I say. But why not?

They've had cats and dogs off and on—they had a cat named Smokey the first summer I was there. Malillie would love it. I offer a corner of my peanut-butter cracker. The kitten eats it, with an exaggerated chomping, and purrs even louder.

"What cave you go in?" he asks suddenly.

"Who, me?" I ask, knowing I sound guilty. "Oh—Paradise. It's—safe." How does he know I've been caving? At once I realize my clothes covered with mud give me away, and the flashlight on my belt.

He doesn't answer. I finish my milk and crackers. He goes in the back and finds me a box that says SHEDD'S SAUCE on it, that will fit in the bike basket. I talk to the kitten all the way home as it mews to get out, clawing at the box with tiny scraping sounds. We beat the rain home.

I guess from the first its name is Treasure.

11

"COME *ON*, MALILLIE!" I URGE HER ALONG IMPATIENTLY. "IT'S A surprise. For you." She follows so slowly, I think. Altogether, I decide, I feel terrific, as if in possession of—well, of an enormous treasure. Tonight the cakewalk—and still, I'm just on the brink of a discovery. It's the feeling you get Christmas Eve, when the tree is lit and the presents are all there, but still wrapped. Malillie seems to feel her way through the murky rooms, through the silent swinging door to the kitchen. I still have plenty of time to get bathed and dressed. "Friday night—cheese sandwiches!" I call out, and my voice sounds as tinkly as a bell. She smells fusty and flowery from the potpourri scattered through drawers and closets. She makes it herself, out of roses, herbs, arrowroot, and things like lemon peel and cloves.

She sits heavily at the kitchen table. "A surprise for me? What in the world—? It's not my birthday yet. Bessie's left us some things to eat. You needn't—"

"I'll start tea first," I say.

"Ah," she sighs, "tea. What would I do if it weren't for tea?"

I put the blue kettle on to boil before retrieving the milky, dust-color kitten from the dusty undercave of the sink and handing it to her, enjoying her wrinkled smile but wondering *why* she has to suddenly act so *old*.

"You found it? It doesn't seem sick or hungry," she says doubtfully, peering to watch the tiny creature stumble on the landscape of her enormous lap. She puts her hand down, and the kitten sniffs it. How much can she see?

"You know how people abandon whole litters. It was all alone in a box at the end of a farm road, well, really right in the fork, when I was out riding." Oh, this is getting worse. Now I am making things up out of whole cloth. I'm shocked to see how easily the lie rolls out of my mouth. *Why* can't I say where I have been? I want to tell her, but not now, not until I know for sure what I've found. Paradise is a long way on a bike—I think it would worry her that I went so far. It's probably eight or ten miles.

I go and look under the overturned bowls to see what Bessie has left: broccoli sodden and limp, and something white and stringy that is probably chicken but smells more like celery. "Yick," I say. "It's definitely a cheese sandwich night." It is a family joke that Bessie is a terrible cook, but she has always believed firmly that cooking is part of her job, and so leaves lukewarm things for us to eat that Graham irreverently calls Car Wreck if they involve tomatoes, or Depressed Chicken or worse.

"Oh, Lee," Malillie says, "you're the devil sent to tempt me. A cheese sandwich sounds divine. . . . Can you catch mice?" she asks the kitten, who is rapelling down her skirt to the floor. "You might come in handy." Treasure wanders

85

over to me, in a not-too-straight line, then back to her. He sniffs the toe of her white shoe, then falls down upon it and lies there, purring loudly, as if to say, *I've chosen you.*

"He's a smart cat," I say, watching him cozying up to the very person who will decide. I go first to the bread box, then to the refrigerator for butter, then to the glass bell that covers the cheese, then to the china cupboard. I've made cheese sandwiches on a plate ever since I noticed mouse droppings on the counter. I take the boiling kettle off the gas and turn to Malillie. "Tea?—or *cocoa?*"

Slowly her face wrinkles up in a grin. "Maybe I need a lift. I've felt so tired today. Will you have a cup too?"

In comes Graham, shaking water off himself. "I'm going to start building an ark tomorrow!" he declares. "Omigod. Where did *she* come from?"

"Someone left it by the roadside," I say, looking at the butter. "She's a he."

"Just what we need," says Graham, rolling his eyes comically. "Looks like it might make a decent stew." He scoops the kitten up and brings it up close in front of his face. The kitten mews. "I reckon not," he says. "All fur, no meat." Treasure mews again and puts a restraining paw on Graham's nose.

I drop a hunk of butter in the skillet, where it sizzles and zigzags across the pan. "Cheese sandwiches," I say. "One or two for you?"

He sniffs the air. "In butter? Two. Maybe three." He dumps the kitten back into Malillie's lap.

"Oh, my goodness," she says, stroking it. "Why are the most helpless creatures always the most attractive?"

I put on the sandwiches I've already made, and slice more cheese, and go to get the cocoa. We are great experts on cocoa, and scorn Hershey's and Nestlé's when we can get more exotic kinds. We love Droste's, but it is too expensive for every day. I always give Malillie a pound for Christmas, as she can't get it in Lavesia. But now it strikes me that we'll be able to have Droste's all the time! The way we like it is just a lot of cocoa and sugar, and boiling water. Not a vitamin in miles, Mama says. But it is balm for the soul, Malillie says. She said once she wasn't sure she believed in vitamins anyway, having never seen one. At home Mama occasionally makes cocoa, but with milk and much less chocolate and sugar. It is, in my estimation, a poor relative.

"He ought to have a name," Graham says, as I flip the sandwiches, and add more butter, lifting them with the spatula so it can melt and run underneath.

Malillie sighs gently. "I *knew* it. Give it a name and it will belong to us forever." Treasure settles deeper into her lap.

"He already has a name," I say. "Treasure."

"Treasure?" Graham asks. "That thing? He'll probably eat us all out of house and home. Why Treasure?"

"Well—he's kind of silvery." I glance up, but Graham hasn't noticed that my voice sounds funny.

He just rolls his eyes and groans, and begins looking through the mail. "Remember the time Horny Lyons tied two cats' tails together so they'd fight, and you spanked his rump with Daddy's razor strap? Boy, you were one tough lady in those days. And always a sap for animals."

"I never did like that Lyons boy, and he never amounted to a thing. I like the name Treasure. Honey, get down the Belleek cups and pot. They make chocolate taste better than anything else!"

I smile, thinking she sounded like Daddy just then.

I pour us all eggshell-thin cups of the black cocoa, and Malillie tastes it and sighs with pleasure. The rest gushes steaming into the tall pot, as glowy as a candled egg, with its shell-like delicacy. Graham pronounces it passable, winking at me. I love this kitchen, these people, this oiled table, the wood translucent-looking, its burns and stains and scratches the ghosts of all the cups and bottles that have spilled and leaked on it for a hundred years. The kitten goes to sleep in Malillie's big lap.

Malillie, as always, moves her fingertips all over the surface of the table. "Mmmm," she says. "Perfect," nodding her white head. I take a sip, and she's right. Then I go and scoop the sandwiches out of the skillet, and cut them catty-cornered with the cheese knife, and take them to the table.

Graham lays the mail down on the floor.

"In Paris," Malillie says slowly, "they always served chocolate this way. Sometimes with whipped cream on top." Graham winks at me across the table. I am endlessly curious about what Malillie was like at my age, so I like stories about her youth. "I remember a café on the Left Bank where they served drinks after the theater, and Hiram and I stopped in one night after the opera when we'd heard Caruso sing in *Faust*." She's silent a moment, smiling at things she can see better, gone fifty years. "We walked over a bridge lit with gas flares, across the Seine from the Opera, and while we drank chocolate some street singers came along, and we threw money to them. One of them had a beautiful monkey." She sighs and takes another sip.

Was she fat then? "Let's all go to Paris," I say, thinking, We *can!*

"Oh, darling, you will, you *will!* That was such a long time ago!" She frowns. "Before Hy and Graham were born, I think . . . "

"Mother," Graham says, "I *hope* it was before we were born. It was your honeymoon."

"Oh, yes," she says. "So it was." She looks sad, and that makes *me* sad.

But Graham says, "We had a cat once named Silver, didn't we, Mama?"

"Not a cat, a dog," she says. "It was the one that turned on Hy and bit him. The county agent came and shot the dog, right in front of Hy. I was furious with the man, but I reckon he had to do it. The dog might have been rabid. Graham, do you remember that? I had to take Hy to Richmond for several weeks."

"Hell, yes, I remember," Graham says. "Hy got to go to the circus, to movies every single night, even to see Blackstone the Magician. And I had to stay here with Pop and go to school every day. Only thing I ever learned at school was what a church key is."

"Oh, Graham," she chides gently, "it wasn't fun. Every morning we had to take the streetcar down to the medical college, and Hy had to have an injection in his belly. He was so nauseated and sore from the shots I don't think he enjoyed any of the things we saw. Not even the circus, and it was Barnum and Bailey, the greatest circus in the world. Twenty-one shots, I think it was. And every day on the streetcar, he'd look so sad, and say, 'I don't want to go today. Don't make me go today.' And I'd say, 'Now you just remember, it'll be over in just a second, and then we'll go to see *Snow White* and have dinner at the Jefferson Hotel.' And he'd say, 'I'll go, but I won't like it.' That was the way he was. 'I'll go, but I won't like it.' "

I try to connect the story with my father now.

"Did the dog have rabies?" I ask, and it comes out in a little voice.

"I can't remember anymore if he did or not. He was dead anyway."

"That's when you got Sport for us. In fact, I think you got him in Richmond. That funny puppy, part Eskimo husky," Graham says. "Ate everything in the house. Pop used to say he must be part Labrador retriever."

Malillie laughs gently. "He ate my best nightgown."

"And a whole box of Brillo pads one time," Graham says. "Remember how he'd bring home the things he stole?"

"A whole beef roast, still hot, if I recall," Malillie says.

"And a toupee," Graham says. "We figured it had to belong to Thom Weston, since he was the only man in Lavesia that wore one."

"But the Westons lived miles from here!" Malillie says.

"You sure couldn't have asked Thom," Graham says. "He flat out denied to the day he died that he wore a toupee. It was entirely a different color than his hair. And he'd put it on two inches different one day from where it had been the day before. People called it Thom's Rug."

"I don't remember whatever happened to Sport," Malillie said. "I forget so much these days. . . ."

She strokes the sleeping kitten in her lap, then she looks up at me with a bright smile. "Your daddy had a hard time as a child. He always took things so seriously. I used to think he married too young, too quickly. . . ." She looks off through the kitchen window, though there is nothing there but blackness, then says, "But my goodness! If he had done differently, we might not have you!"

"I guess some people just don't know when they're lucky," I say, and smile. But Malillie acts like she didn't hear, just stares away into the darkness. Then she says, "I think maybe we have to make allowances."

90

I feel a little uncomfortable. Malillie looks at her lap where the kitten is, and Graham stretches and rubs his hand over his head. "What a day!" he says loudly. "You know, I can't fix that damn stove of Harold's. I had to call Roanoke to order a new oven door, and the guy delivered it today and it doesn't fit. Now what the hell am I going to do?"

"If it's not worth fixing, don't try to fix it," Malillie says slowly.

"Oh, I know, I know," Graham says, "I tried telling that to Harold. But people think they can save money . . . any dessert around?"

I shake my head. "I was going to make something for you today, but I got back from riding too late. I'll make it tomorrow."

"You went riding today? In this rain? Are you crazy? You didn't used to be crazy. But then I reckon you didn't used to be a teenager, either."

"I have to get exercise, don't I? It wasn't raining then, anyway."

"How long have you practiced the piano this summer?" he asked.

"About the same as last summer," I admit. I sigh and roll my eyes upward. "Last summer was my piano phase. I'm in my biking phase this year."

Graham shakes his head. "Then come on, I'll carry you ladies down the road to the Dari-Queen for dessert."

"Oh, I can't," I say. "Hunter's coming to take me to the cakewalk, and I have to get ready." Then I grin at him joyously. "Someday, Graham, I'm going to be rich, and when I am, I'll buy you a Dari-Queen of your own. Or a candy store. Or both. You and Malillie enjoy yourselves."

Malillie doesn't, as she usually does, respond happily. In

91

fact, Graham and I catch each other's eyes watching her, waiting for her to respond.

"Mother?" Graham asks finally.

"Yes?" Her voice sounds—blurry.

"Graham's going to take you to the Dari-Queen," I say.

But she shakes her head. In her lap, Treasure sleeps, curled as tight as a boiled shrimp. "Too tired. You two go, have—good—time."

Then she seems to rouse herself a little, or at least her voice is clearer. "Graham, I'm so tired tonight. I'll turn in, I think. Just bring me that cocoa pot and I'll see if I can squeeze another drop out of it."

"Are you sure you're all right, Mother?" Graham asks, frowning. Malillie nods gently, her eyes nearly closed. "Bessie's going to be furious when she sees what we've done to her kitchen."

She leans on the table, trying to get up. I am just reaching to help her when she falls forward to the floor, spilling the kitten. Her fall unbalances one of the Belleek cups, which rolls over and off the table, shattering on the floor right beside her.

12

DR. CARTER FINALLY GETS AROUND TO ME. "WHAT'S WRONG?" I ASK, not really wanting to hear, a knot of pain gathering in my stomach. *I* fed her cheese sandwiches and rich hot chocolate for supper, urging her to eat more, drink more. Graham's still in the sitting room with her.

"Ah, just a spell, some confusion, something that happens when you get old," says Dr. Carter. "I don't think it's too serious." But then, looking at my face, he puts a hand on my shoulder. "Don't give up on your grandmother yet. She's got plenty of gristle. She just needs rest and a little looking after. You're the best medicine she's got."

I want to know more, but Hunter arrives at this point, his hair still slick from a shower. I had forgotten all about him.

Dr. Carter shakes his hand silently, asks after his father, then inquires if he's been fishing lately. They compare notes on a couple of holes in the river where there are supposed to be big trout.

When Dr. Carter has gone, Hunter and I stand alone in the hall. "I don't think I want to go to a cakewalk," I say.

He nods. It's all right. "Is Miss Lillie going to be okay?"

"I don't know," I say. "Dr. Carter called it a *spell.*"

"That's an improvement," he says. "Usually he calls it the grippe."

"He calls *what* the grippe?"

"Whatever you got wrong with you," Hunter says.

"*Spell* doesn't tell you much either," I say.

"Yeah. That makes it sound like somebody hexed her," he says.

"Hexed her?" A scary thought enters my head. Out of habit we are moving toward the kitchen. "You believe in that kind of stuff?"

"No. I was just talking."

But I'm thinking. Shakespeare put a curse on anyone bothering his bones. So did King Tut, and look what happened. My upper arms have sprouted gooseflesh. "Do you think it's possible?" Could there be a curse on the Beale Treasure, or, rather, on anyone who disturbs it?

But Hunter has turned me around by the shoulders, and his face is close. "What's the matter with you? You're just upset. Nobody would hex Miss Lillie."

Now is the moment. I want to tell him. I don't know why I can't. He says, very gently, "She's not young. The Lord may be thinking it's time—"

I turn sharply away, not wanting to hear. "You want something to drink?"

He hesitates, then says to my back, "I reckon I ought not to stay just now."

But I turn back to him. "No—Hunter—please—don't go yet. I'll make lemonade."

He nods assent. I ask about his mother and father, and Ned, his brother, and his family, and Eugene, the middle one, who has his own service station now, at Maple Hill. It's Eugene's motorcycle Hunter was going to borrow to take me to the cakewalk on. I reckon it's outside.

When he asks about the winter, and Drew and Gee, and what-all's happened since I was here last, I find myself among other things telling about the night in Suzanne's ghost room.

"So—no ghost?" he asks, when I'm through.

"No," I say, and smile.

For a moment he doesn't say anything. Then he says, "I had a girl friend last winter."

I have to steel myself not to react. "You did?" I say.

"Uh-huh," he says, nodding. "Course didn't anyone see her but me."

"What do you mean?"

"Well," he says, "She was a girl. A young girl. She woke me up every night for a while. She felt just like a real person, pinching my feet or pulling the covers off me."

"Wait a minute," I say. "What do you mean? She wasn't real?"

"I don't know," he says. "I'd turn on the light, and wouldn't anybody be there. Just me, alone in the room."

Relief floods me. "Hunter!" I say. "So what happened?" Yet I can identify jealousy in myself.

He clasps his hands in front of him. "There are spirits in the Bible," he says. "I—told my folks about it. In fact, we were having Sunday dinner after church. Ned and Nancy and their kids were there, too, and I just told everyone. Said I didn't know what to do, she was disturbing my sleep every night. I don't even know how I knew it was a girl. I don't know what she looked like, just what she *was*. So finally Ma says, kind of laughing, 'Whyn't you *ask* her next time what she wants.'

"Just at that time I hear this *thump* on the ceiling right overhead, right up where my room is. Sounded—kind of mad. I look around to see if anyone else heard it, but everyone else just keeps on eating. I knew it was *her,* and I knew she was hurt that I told. It was like she'd wanted me to keep it a secret. And just then Teddy, Ned's little one, looked up and said, 'What was that noise?' And everyone else said, 'What noise?' and 'I didn't hear anything' and like that. And you know, that was the end of that."

"You never got waked up again?"

"Nope. And now I don't know if I imagined the whole thing. Except Teddy heard."

"That's crazy," I say. But I hope secretly she'll stay away and let him alone.

And now is the time for me to share with him what I've found, so I lean across the table and say, "Hunter—" just as Graham comes through the door, preceded by a bounding

95

Treasure. Of course I ask if I can go in and see Malillie, and is she all right, and Graham says sure, I can go have a peek, and that he knows I won't wake her up. Then he turns to Hunter and asks him about the farm.

When I come back, Hunter's lemonade glass stands empty on the table, and Graham explains he thought it best to go on home. Graham has a bottle of whiskey and a cheese glass sitting on the table, and he looks tired. "Graham, she'll be okay, won't she?" I ask.

He nods, slowly. "Sure, hon," he says, and pours a half-glass of whiskey for himself. "You want a drink?" he says. "You're old enough for a drink."

Flattered out of my mind, I say, "Sure," careful to sound casual. So I get a glass and he pours me some. But at the first taste, I cough and my throat burns, and I have to admit it's awful. Graham just grins his amusement at me, and finishes my glass himself. I offer to stay with Malillie, but Graham sends me to bed, saying he wants to do it.

Monday, June 19

13

FOR THREE DAYS I HAVE BEEN A TEA-CARRIER, BACK AND FORTH, back and forth from the kitchen to Malillie's room: teapots ginger red and gold Cantonese, with little Chinese people on them going along a road to market, carrying things on their backs and heads; blue and white Delft, two lovers holding hands on a windy bridge over a canal, the girl's skirts blowing, a windmill behind them. Has Hunter ever held my hand? Why is it that I can't remember? He must have, walking in a precarious spot or getting up a slippery bank, but I can't remember. I guess it didn't *mean* anything. I sigh, go back to studying the teapots. This one is heavy and homely, brown stoneware. I know about china from Malillie, I suddenly realize. All her life she has named its names, and told me about it. Stoneware rings when hit, earthenware does not. Here is a pot of pink English Worcester ware. Ground bone is added to make the china translucent. Malillie has dozens of teapots, and each one is as loved as a pet.

In Lavesia, company comes when there is sickness. Eliza Triplett has twice walked up the hill to sit a spell. She and Malillie have been friends since girlhood. Mrs. Triplett has been a widow for forty years. They have been widows together since before I was born. Dr. Carter has been back every day. His wife came yesterday with a still-warm custard. Others. Even Jerry Dunne.

Hunter came back awhile last night after church, bringing a big box of strawberries. Three neighbors were there, including Harold and Norma Simmons. Of course we didn't mention the stove, and I couldn't take Hunter aside to talk. One by one they all stopped in to speak to Malillie. I made two big pitchers of iced tea, and crushed mint into them. Hunter, never one to overstay his welcome, got up shortly and walked out into the soft darkness, and I felt like running after him, but of course I didn't, with people all over the porch.

And the rain: it has continued, off and on. Malillie has rested, slept, awakened to eat some custard or drink some tea, to talk to some neighbor. "I wanted to do the preserves with you," she said apologetically this morning, "but strawberries won't wait."

So this morning Bessie is "doing" the berries friends have brought, and the house smells of preserves, that sweet, hot summer smell that is like no other. "Fast high heat keeps the flavor better than slow cooking," Malillie said, "but then you have to stir. So nowadays I do them slow so I can rest a little bit." Everything she says seems to me heavy with meaning. Her hands fall uselessly onto the sheet.

Nothing in the three days could be called alarming, though once, waking up, she mumbled it was time to go home. I began to feel afraid, thinking she meant heaven, but then she continued, saying Paris was lovely, but it really was time to go. "Malillie," I said, "you're home." And she gazed unseeing at the ceiling and said, "How strange. I was dreaming. I was young. I could even smell the market in Paris. Les

Halles. At night all the workmen from all over Paris would come off duty and go to Les Halles and eat onion soup in the little restaurants. Or fried smelts."

Late last night Dr. Carter came again, and said her blood pressure was low, that there was nothing to do but wait. And once again, I feared that by disturbing the treasure, or trying to, that I might have unbalanced something.

But this morning, she seems so nearly her old self that I realize how foolish that idea is. Things don't have mysterious power over people.

So now I sit in the kitchen, thinking maybe Graham was right when he said it would rain all summer. When will I get a chance to get back out there and open one of the pots?

I get out milk for Treasure. I look at Bessie's back, hoping I can taste soon, hold a spoonful of the preserves to see if the two droplets of syrup will merge into one and hang, motionless as a ruby, on the edge of the spoon. I feel jumpy, and I know I need to get out and do something.

Treasure laps milk up frantically, stepping in the dish in his haste, then shaking his feet helplessly. I chop up some cheese for him, which he eats while I make myself a pot of coffee. Then he tries gracelessly to wash his face, and gives up, busying himself trying to kill the already-ragged hem of my dressing gown.

I look at the kitchen clock for the umpteenth time. It must be broken; it isn't moving at all. I feel I've been waiting for weeks for Malillie to get up out of bed so I can relax.

Treasure decides to climb the screen door to the porch, and gets stuck, spread-eagled, hollering for help. "Out," Bessie says, pushing at the screen. But he dives inward, and heads for the pantry as fast as he can go, and the door bangs shut again.

99

"Guess he doesn't want to get wet," I say.

"Reckon," she says.

"Bessie, did Malillie ever have a spell like this one before?"

"Seems like she did," Bessie says, stirring like a witch from *Macbeth*.

I can't go into the sitting room again. Not yet. "I don't guess you'd like to play cards?"

"What cards?" she says, still stirring.

"Oh, I don't know. War. Crazy Eight. Ninety-nine. Anything you want."

"Law, child, I ain't ever heard of them."

I miss Gee and Drew. I wish they were here to play Fish or Old Maid. Parcheesi, even, and I hate Parcheesi. I wish somebody would write to me. It seems to me much longer than two weeks since I saw them. Barbara. Camille. What are they up to?

Treasure, on the screen again, falls to the floor, gets up shakily like Wile E. Coyote, then bounds across the floor. Drew would love Treasure. Gee would need to be scornful, loyal to his future dog. I really do miss them. And Mama. I see her, tired and kind of sad, still in her nightgown when I get home from school, waiting for me to take over so she can bathe and dress.

Itchy and restless as I am, I don't want to leave the house, not until I know Malillie is all right. I wonder what Hunter is doing this morning. Graham said he is going to work after lunch. One of Jerry Dunne's kids, Amy, seventeen or eighteen, is keeping the store this morning. I offered to, but Graham says Amy knows where everything is. Usually in Lavesia, people just put up a sign, BACK AFTER LUNCH, or CLOSED TODAY. COME BACK TO-MORROW. Graham hardly ever takes off.

I knock lightly on the sitting-room door, and when there's no answer, I open it. Graham looks up, peering over his thick glasses, putting his finger to his mouth. He has yesterday's *New York Times* still spread out around him like dead leaves. He goes to Tatum's every Sunday to pick it up. The blinds are drawn except behind the chair where Graham's sitting, but I can see that Malillie moves, first a hand, then her head, just enough to reassure me she's alive. Graham has worked his way through a pile of *Sportscar* magazines and a couple of dozen doughnuts in a white waxed bag with a cellophane window. How he stays thin I'll never know. I close the door softly.

I write a second letter to Gee and Drew, and tell them about Treasure. There's not much else. I talk about the weather, and tell them to write me the news. I just can't tell them about the treasure, though I'm dying to. Mama will read the letter, and she'd tell Daddy, and God only knows what would happen then.

I start into a pile of old *National Geographics* they keep stacked in the bottom of one of the bookcases, and see that the world is made up of infinite numbers of strange, sometimes unexplainable things. I stare for a long time at pictures, in two different articles, of strange rock formations. One of them is almost exactly like a naked woman leaning back on her elbow and is called The Petrified Woman; another looks like a huge, artistically carved head, though the explanation says it was entirely "carved" by wind and erosion.

Finally I find a deck of cards on the sideboard, and deal a hand of Las Vegas solitaire. At least it's the way Graham says they play in Las Vegas: they sell you a deck of cards for a dollar apiece, or $52, then give you $5 back for every card you extract from the deck. It seems like you couldn't lose. You need only get back eleven of the fifty-two cards to be ahead, that is, to make $55. Since he told me that, I've always kept track of how much I win or lose, and I never cheat. Yet now I am $1267 in the hole. I've kept the records for three years now, and I've only won once, in what must be a couple hundred games. I think that this is a good thing to remember in case I am ever tempted to gamble. I sigh as I add another $27 to my loss.

I wander back to the kitchen just as Bessie takes the preserves off the heat. Treasure jumps on my foot, and I lift him to my lap. "Bessie," I say firmly, feeling him purr through his soft coat, "what would you do if you found the Beale Treasure?"

"Me," she says. "Law!" She shakes her head. "Prolly scorch these here preserves, to begin."

"I'm serious," I say. "Really. What would you do?" Treasure gnaws on my hand while his back feet bicycle against it furiously.

Bessie is silent a long time. I think I'll get out the bike and ride out there, to check on the pots. But every time I think of doing that, I figure that what has sat there 150 years can wait another day or two. "Buy me a car and drive up this hill to work, that's what. Then I give it out, all the rest, to the blacks in this area, and we have a party last all weekend long."

"What I mean is, would you tell anyone?"

With tongs, she removes jelly glasses from hot water. She is so silent I begin to think she hasn't heard, or isn't going to answer. "No white people," she says finally.

"How come?"

" 'Cause white people wouldn't let no coloreds keep no money like that."

"Yeah. I reckon that's right," I say.

"I know it's right. Gubmint won't even let me keep the money your gran'mother pay me."

I watch her ladle the hot preserves into six small glasses, and am disappointed, as after missing some important ritual. "How do you know they're done?"

"I don't know," she says. "How you know if you're in love?"

How indeed? "Can I lick the pot?" I ask.

After lunch Graham leaves for the store. I slip quietly into Malillie's room and sit beside her. Finally she stirs, struggling toward waking. "Malillie," I whisper, "I think I've found the Beale Treasure."

In half-sleep, she tries to speak, her mouth moving. Finally, she struggles upright. "Treasure was a great find," she says, and her voice is firm.

"Oh, yes!" I say, eager now to unburden myself, to share it with her.

"A merry heart doeth more good than medicine," she says smiling warmly. "Everyone needs a pet."

At first I am confused. Then I sit back. She thinks I am talking about the cat! "I believe I'm going to live," she says. "I'm *hungry*. You know what I'd like? Just a small piece of coconut custard pie. Don't you think you or Bessie could manage that, darling?"

14

THE AFTERNOON SUN IS WARM ON MY HAIR. HUGGING THE BROWN bag of groceries that Malillie has requested from Fox's, I come upon the trailer in the parking lot on the corner. I'd forgotten the county Bookmobile comes to Lavesia Monday afternoons. Skidding to a stop, I prop the bike outside, and the groceries I set crackling down on the sunny trailer step. I'll just stay a second, get Malillie a book.

The librarian looks up, carefully puts a paper marker in the book she's reading, and frowns, repeating my question thoughtfully, wondering aloud if they have anything on the truck about that. I say, "It doesn't really matter. I just wondered, was all."

But she shoves up the sleeves of her beige sweater and says, "No, it's an interesting question. I'd like to know myself. I never thought about it. Hmmm. If you found a treasure—" She looks up at me. "You mean, like the Beale Treasure?"

I feel my heart flop over like a desperate fish, but I manage to sound careless when I answer, "I guess so."

"Yes," she says. "Who *would* it belong to? Wait here a minute."

I do my best to look halfway between bored and interested and say again that it doesn't matter, really, not to worry about it. I tell myself that no matter what the answer is, I am never going back there again. *Let Malillie stay well and I won't fool with fate anymore . . .* maybe her "spell" was a warning.

The librarian goes over to the back, and returns in a minute with a huge book, dark red. I help her hoist it to the table inside the trailer door. It has very tiny printing. She chats, running her finger down an index page. "I don't know why no one ever asked before, when we've got such a famous treasure buried somewhere right around here." And she laughs merrily, as if it's very funny. She turns some pages. "Aren't you Lillie Eldridge's granddaughter?"

Startled, I want to deny it, to remain anonymous. But she looks up questioningly at me, so I have to say, "Oh, yes." Guilty. My cover blown. She lifts a heavy mass of pages, and the thick spine of the book shifts. She begins to leaf backward. "How is she these days? We've missed her. She hasn't been in for some time."

"Uh, fine, thanks."

"And your uncle?"

"Fine."

"Good!" she says. "Tell Mrs. Eldridge we've got some new talking books that are real nice, will you? Maybe you'd like to take her one. Ah, here we are. 'In Virginia law,' " she reads, " 'treasure belongs to the finder: thus, if a man hires another to look for gold or minerals on his land, and the hiree finds buried treasure, it is the property of the hirer. If the hiree finds the gold looked for in a vein or rock on the hirer's property, it is the hirer's, the land and intent belonging to him. However, if a man hires another to dig a well on his property, or anything of the sort having nothing to do with minerals or metals, and the hiree should find buried treasure, it is the hiree's, according to Gray *vs.* Malone 1903.' Treasure in Virginia law does not belong to the land."

Which leaves me still holding the pots, so to speak. Sometimes I try to imagine them lined up in Malillie's parlor. How will I get them out? What should I do? Will reporters come? Will thieves? What would my father do?

I just can't figure what would happen. I picture myself, my canvas bookbag emptied of math and spelling and leftover lunch and library books, instead sagging with gold and silver coins out of a fairy tale, climbing the broad steps of a big museum somewhere, in some city, trying to sell them or something. What would happen next? I try to imagine coming back down the steps, bookbag stuffed with dollar bills, like when we go to Dan Womack's garden in the summertime to pick lettuce. I can't convince myself of any of it.

I leave with a collection of ghost stories and a recorded

book, *The Silver Chalice,* for Malillie. "I love to read anything sensational," I tell the lady, hoping this will somehow explain my bizarre interest in treasure.

My route home takes me right by the store. I find Graham squatted like an enormous grasshopper on the floor, trying to fit a new door onto Harold Simmons's stove. He's painted over the chipped enamel, but it still looks like a fixed, wrecked stove. "It looks better," I say encouragingly.

Graham just shakes his head. "Waste of money. He should have left Norma twenty years ago. That hinny is so mean she'd make Genghis Khan look like a pussycat. I was in high school with her." He rolls his eyes as if that explains everything. He taps the hinges with a hammer, but the two parts won't fall together. "Shoot!" he says. "I give up. Like trying to put socks on a rooster." He stands up, and wipes sweat from his face with a handkerchief. "It's a shame," he goes on. "Here you've been here two weeks already, isn't it?—and we haven't gotten you inside a cave yet. We'll try to go Sunday, if Mama's okay. Only you have to promise not to scare me to death again—or worse, *starve* me to death—"

I shake my head at him. "You're crazy," I tell him. "I have to go now. Malillie's starving, and asked me to get a bunch of things."

Graham looks up. "You're a peach, hon. Don't know what we'd do without you." He blows me a kiss as I leave, the doorbell tinkling.

PART II

Finders keepers
Losers weepers.
—*Mother Goose* rhyme

Wednesday, June 21

15

I DIDN'T TAKE ANYTHING BUT THE RING. IT IS HARD TO BELIEVE THAT one measly ring could cause so much trouble.

It is as if nature knows what is going to happen in advance, and is getting wound up for it, because I've no more than set out on Graham's bicycle that day, with a hammer and a screwdriver smuggled inside my rolled-up nylon jacket, when the wind starts. At first, it is just a brisk breeze, but by the time I've ridden all the way out to Paradise Mountain it's whipping leaves off the trees and hurling them in my face, and the sky has hunkered and lowered until it reminds me of someone huge, and mad, maybe God, squatting there angrily right on top of the mountain. I've never seen such wind, and I try to comfort myself with the memory of what Malillie said: this is not tornado country. Her voice is strong and steady again, and even Graham insisted, when I worried aloud, that it was just a spell and nothing serious.

If it wasn't such a long trip, I'd turn around and go back, nonetheless. I don't like wind. But once I'm there, I look up the mountain toward the cave and I can't *not* stay. I put on my jacket against the blowing leaves and bark, and once I am inside the cave there is an instant calm, as if a lid has dropped on the world. All I can hear is the soft dripping of the water, and not the whipping sounds of the wind. It is very peaceful. I think for an instant of Malillie, alone with Bessie in the house that is, after all, on top of a hill. She seems very far away, though I know I could get to her in half an hour. Just a spell. Nothing serious. She agreed with Graham that I must "do something for myself." In fact, she said, "Darling, if I looked as pert as I feel, you'd be looking at Gloria Swanson," by which I saw she really was her old self again.

I tell myself I won't stay but ten minutes in the cave. And that this is not tornado country.

I go back to that third pot, because it looks to me that it is going to be the easiest. And I work at it until the top breaks loose, scattering rust down the sides onto my shoes, and I lift it off carefully and shine my light in.

Somewhere you've seen a treasure like this, in an old movie, or maybe in a dream. Or in your mind as someone read a fairy tale like "Ali Baba and the Forty Thieves" or the story in *The Jungle Book* where Mowgli finds a great treasure guarded by a white cobra. That is what it looks like.

The first thing the flashlight gleam shows is a ring. It is lying there among some leather bags and coins and gold chains, and my light lands right on it. It takes my breath away and fires that flashlight gleam right back at me, winking and saying, *Take* me, take *me*. So I do, I don't know why. Not to show anyone. Not to sell. Not to wear, certainly. Just—for a token, maybe.

Anyway, I take it, and put it on my middle finger and close the pot, jamming the lid back on quickly. I feel afraid. The ring, too big, slides around the instant I get it on, and I can feel the heavy stone dragging down into my palm, and a coldness where it lies. I scoot, clinging spiderlike to it, around the slick boulder, and leave quickly, a little worried about Malillie, nudged by guilt at having left her.

Nothing shows of my visit but a shiny gray shank over my middle finger. Dirt and leaves swirl up in imitation of the tornadoes we don't have as I crash down the mountain, not stopping to examine the ring.

On the road rocks scatter up in my face as if thrown by an unseen hand, and the bike wobbles. I ride the whole way with my hair lashing around crazily and my eyes squinted shut to where I just barely can see out between the lashes. All the time I have the uncomfortable feeling that someone is watching, or following, pulling me back or shoving me forward roughly, though it is perfectly certain that no one but me is here. I keep telling myself to be sensible; that I've read too many ghost stories. I plan a hiding place for the ring, then another, my mind leaping from room to room in Malillie's house, opening drawers, choosing then rejecting scores of places. And I think up my story just in case someone does find it.

Once, halfway home, for just an instant the clouds part and some sun falls on and around me. I stop the bike in the road, wipe my glasses clean, and turn the ring over. It's absolutely stunning, the diamond as wide as my finger, set in a raised old-fashioned filigree of silver or platinum or white gold. I move it from underneath with my thumb and it winks rainbow: orange and gold and yellow and grass-green and emerald. It is the most elegant ring I've ever seen. Then abruptly the sun goes in, swallowed by some more whipped up clouds, and the rain smell comes strong at me.

16

WHEN I GET HOME, RIGHT NECK AND NECK WITH THE STORM, MY blouse spattered with dark spots, the first thing has already happened. The wind, Bessie reports. It had blown so hard it shattered the big glass pane in the top half of the kitchen door, and she is sweeping up shards of glass into the dustpan while the curtains flap inward, with nothing to stop them.

"Where you been?" She doesn't wait for an answer, but says, "You go call Mr. Graham, tell him bring some new glass for the back door when he come home from work."

"Is Malillie all right?"

"Yep. She's just fine."

As I walk through the door to the pantry, my foot lands *c-crack* on a piece of glass that has skidded all the way there. I bend down and pick up the two pieces, and go on through the dining room to the hall where the telephone is. Somewhere I hear a door bang, and the descending rush of the rain.

The phone isn't working. There is a crackling on the line. I stand, listening to static, and slip the ring off my finger. I cradle the phone on my shoulder, with one hand holding the ring and the other holding a piece of the glass. *L*, I scratch with the stone. *Zzzt. Tzzz.* Oh, easy. Then an *E: zzzt.* And *zit zit zit*. All there is to it. It's *real* diamond. The line buzzes and sounds funny. Outside a tree crashes against the house.

"Honey, what are you doing?"

I whirl around. I haven't heard anyone coming. Guiltily I close the ring and glass in the palm of my hand, and feel a quick pain as one of the pieces of glass cuts in. "Oh, I'm just calling Graham," I say. My hand is still closed, and I hold it against my chest.

"I was just coming to see if you'd gotten home. I was worried to death about you, out in all this storm," she says. "Isn't it the fiercest weather?" She puts her hand over mine and squeezes.

"Ow!" I cry, jerking away.

"Oh, darling! I'm so sorry! What in the world—?" For my hand has opened of its own accord to show the glass shard, ring, and blood all together, though the hall is nearly dark and Malillie is nearly blind. "Your hand—it's bleeding!" she says, then, "My gracious, where did *this* come from?"

I have to stay there and watch her take the ring and peer closely at it, turning it this way and that.

"It's just a fake, Malillie," I say. "It's costume jewelry. I got it for nearly nothing. The glass in it cut me, I guess, when you squeezed my hand."

"How dreadful!" she says. "Let's get some alcohol. Where did you get it? Downtown?"

"Oh, no—a place in Richmond—a junk shop."

She looks puzzled. "Were you wearing it just now?"

I'm cornered. And I do a terrible thing. "Don't you remember?" I ask. "I told you I'd gotten it for your birthday present—just because it was pretty—and you asked to see it. The other day, when you were sick." Outside the wind howls.

"Oh," she says softly, sadly. "Of course. It's gorgeous, darling."

"For junk, it's okay," I say, feeling awful.

"Hang up the phone, and let's fix your hand."

"It's really okay," I tell her. "I don't think the phone's working at all. The pane in the back door broke."

"The storm probably blew the line down," Malillie says. Suddenly, somewhere upstairs, something cracks, then crashes. The house shakes. It isn't a door slamming.

113

Upstairs.

Without thinking, I leap toward the stairs, with Malillie following, clumsy as an elephant. At the top of the stairs, I stop short. A white mist rolls upward and out, like a wave, from the door of my room. I stare at it, then back at Malillie, still struggling to climb the stairs. The weight of the ring clings to my finger like a nagging child, and my palm is sticky with blood. I want to get somewhere to clean up the ring and look at it carefully.

My room lies in a white fog, the entire ceiling having collapsed in jagged chunky layers on the bed, the chair, the dresser, the dark floor, the shelf of odd dolls and books and stuffed animals. Big Bear, a grayish dog Daddy had when he was a boy, lies against my pillow, against blue homespun, looking out from between two boulders of plaster. I follow his blank button gaze upward to the ceiling. Lathing meets my eyes, and dust rises in the air to about our shoulder height, and hangs there.

"I knew it would happen someday," Malillie says. She sounds sad. "Little pieces fall all the time," she adds. "The damn wind!" she says, and I have never heard her swear before.

But the ring still hangs on my sticky finger, and I turn it over and look at it, and even blood-smeared it gives me a solemn, evil wink of white light, drawn from some source I can't see. It is the damn ring, I think, and feel the hair on the back of my neck bristle.

"Law!" Bessie says, behind us. "What a mess!"

"I think you'll have to move to another room for a while," Malillie tells me.

Bessie trudges slowly downstairs for a broom, muttering. Malillie stands shapeless and helpless in her hall, and seems to be staring in the direction of my hand.

114

"I couldn't think what you'd like for your birthday," I say.

"You shouldn't have gotten me anything!" she says, sounding pleased.

"I really *meant* to keep it a secret until then." But I don't like this. I'm afraid of what will happen if she wears it.

"Well, honey, you just pretend I didn't see it." Outside the rain just pours.

Bessie comes struggling back up with the vacuum cleaner, and I go to help her. "Kitchen door needs fixing bad," she says. "Rain and leafs just pouring in. Look like that whole storm trying to dump itse'f in your kitchen."

Both of them turn imploring eyes to me. The phone isn't working. They hate for me to go out in this, but the lightning has stopped. It's ten minutes at most, all downhill, to the store, and Graham will drive me back up in a minute. BACK IN FIFTEEN MINUTES. He'll have no customers in this weather anyway.

"Okay," I sigh. "Let me get a raincoat."

I drop the ring in the pocket of a shift hanging near the raincoat in the closet. It falls silently to the bottom of the pocket, and I feel unburdened to have it off. I stop by the bathroom to wash my hands until no sign of the blood is left, just a tiny straight cut, a wayside lane among the other life-lines and fate lines that cross my palm and each other, going God knows where. In the mirror a streak of drying blood cuts down my cheek. I wash it away too.

Halfway down the drive, wind and rain tear the hood from my head. As I reach up to pull it back on, the bike skids, and even before I take the rain full on my face and hear my own gasp, or feel the jarring crash, I know, with the drama of a lightning bolt and the certainty of the thunder that follows, that the ring has unleashed all of this.

115

Thursday, June 22

17

BY THE TIME I MAKE IT BACK UP TO THE HOUSE, THE STORM IS OVER, but I can't ride into town because my shoulder's killing me. So when Graham gets home, he takes me over to Dr. Carter's, dropping Bessie off on the way and picking up a pane of glass at the store. The old doctor pokes at my shoulder and makes me move it, and says it looks to be a sprain, that he's sure nothing is broken. Aspirin, he says, ice on the shoulder, and rest until it feels better.

In addition, I have managed to chill myself to the bone.

In wet or cold weather the upstairs is always cold. There's no insulation in the house. One of Daddy's favorite comments when Graham goes to Atlanta or New York: "He has no business doing that. He ought to spend that money getting the house insulated!" So I stand it up there as long as I can, not even in my own room, but in a soft sagging bed in a strange shadowy back bedroom Malillie uses as a storeroom: Chinese screens and boxes full of books and a table with more boxes on it. Red-orange dragons float or crawl on the screen, twisting and writhing. Could that be where my child-hood dragons had come from? There's a locked desk with a

116

bronze bust of someone on it, and a dusty American flag fringed in gold propped in a corner. Faded daguerreotypes hang on the wall; oval in square frames. It all reminds me some way of Graham's back room at the store. I fall asleep with Treasure on my chest, and as I sleep it seems I enter a dark musty store in the city, the sun falling through suspended dust motes, a marble bust on a table halfway back, piles of boxes, a daybed with a white cat asleep on it, a counter of glass with jewelry under it, the owner saying, "Let me show you this." Ghosts watch me from the walls. And he brings out a cigar box with a nearly bald man portrayed there, and inside the box is my ring, a gold bracelet, a turquoise figure which he says is an Egyptian god of death, some marbles, and a necklace with stones the color of tea with milk. It is all so clear I could have named the color of every marble. I bring out two dollar bills to pay for the ring, and awake remembering.

And when I try to think of the treasure, how three times I have seen the pots, once opened one, that seems less believable than the dream I have just dreamed.

I sit up, blowing my nose and shivering, and come downstairs where it is warmer. Malillie, distressed at my injury, now presses tea on me as I did her only a few days back. She blames herself for letting me go out in the storm.

And I continue to wonder if all these things happening at once can be coincidental. In one moment, I am bravely scornful of any other explanation; the next I am sure that occult forces are at work in the world.

Malillie and I play canasta and rummy, and at some point I decide I must get the ring out of the house. I can't give it to Malillie for her birthday. There is no point in taking chances by keeping it around.

The day outside is colorless and as dark as twilight when Hunter arrives, with a big bunch of wild flowers. He has picked the bouquet: white Queen Anne's lace, orange poppies, blue chicory, goldenrod. At once I begin to sneeze.

"You allergic? I thought you weren't allergic to anything!" He looks so chagrined I have to laugh.

"I caught cold yesterday. They're beautiful. How'd you know to come?"

"I heard last night at church. Mrs. Carter said you'd been by earlier to see the doc, that you'd hurt your shoulder. I would have been by sooner, but the rain washed a gutter off the house, and I've been trying to fix it. That storm yesterday rained a blacksnake right down into the house. It was curled up in the kitchen this morning. Seemed to like it there. Didn't want to leave."

My heart lifts. It was just the wind, the storm. "You ought to see what it did to my room," I say. "Come on, I'll show you."

"Can you walk okay?"

"Hunter," I say, "I don't walk on my shoulders." Then I'm sorry, because he takes his hand away.

"I can fix that up in no time," he says, surveying the ceiling. "I'll come tomorrow or the next day."

"You don't have time to do that!" I protest.

"Sure I do," he says. "What's a neighbor for?"

"You know who you look like today?" I ask.

"Robert Redford?" he asks, hopefully.

"Will Rogers. I was reading an article about him in a *National Geographic* the other day."

"Will Rogers would have liked me," he says.

"How come?"

"He said he never met a man he didn't like," Hunter says,

grinning. "But I kind of thought I looked like Robert Redford. *Mama* thinks I look like Robert Redford."

"The ugly one in all those cowboy movies? *That* Robert Redford?"

"That's the one." His voice is deep and resonant and sure now, after two summers of playing odd scales. Every time he speaks I'm surprised.

"I'm not sure I like you anymore," I tell him lightly.

He looks amused at that. "Oh, sure you do," he says.

"Well, I still think you look like Will Rogers," I say. "But the *flowers* are pretty."

Yesterday seems like a bad dream. Treasure attacks my hand, purring like mad. Hunter is here. Malillie comes in with cocoa and cookies. I could tell the two of them, here in this secure room, about what I found. So what makes me hesitate? Malillie asks, won't Hunter stay for supper? "You're looking so much better," Malillie tells me.

"If I looked as good as I feel, you'd be looking at Farrah Fawcett-Majors," I say, winking at Hunter. He rolls his eyes.

"Who in the world is that?" Malillie asks. She stoops to pick up Treasure, who has stepped onto the tea tray. "Don't want you breaking up my Crownware," she says, putting him on her lap. Treasure leaps off and skitters sideways across the floor, escaping hallucinated enemies. And I never want to be anywhere else than here, in this room, at this time.

119

Friday, June 23

18

I AWAKEN, FEEL TO SEE IF MY SHOULDER STILL HURTS. MAYBE A LIT-tle, but the world this morning seems okay again. The sun is shining, birds sing—

Then I remember what I vowed to do. I will not eat breakfast until it is done. I am going to get rid of it.

Guarding my shoulder, I dress in the shift that has the ring in the pocket. I don't want to touch it again. The cleanup job in my room isn't finished yet. White plaster dust still shows in the cracks of the wooden floor, and above, holes like caves lead into the darkness of the attic. I don't like the idea that there could be someone up there watching me. I shiver and look over my shoulder. I move gingerly, as it seems that the least motion is the best thing, for both the ring and me. No jarring, my mind cautions. Don't stir up any more storms. My shoulder twinges warningly, as if reverberations might begin that could cause Lord only knows how much more evil. Yet I feel sad to throw away such a thing of concentrated beauty, concentrated value. I don't know its worth, but it might buy a new car for Graham, a new house, a trip to Paris, a new heart for Malillie! A million fried cheese sandwiches!

120

Buried things can be dug up, but if I drop it off the high bridge into the James River below, no one will ever be able to recover it; but mostly, it will be beyond temptation for me. It will roll slowly downstream, tumbling, bury itself awhile in silt, then wash free again, moving through green countryside, past Richmond in a few thousand years, into the Chesapeake Bay in a few million, and on to the ocean, where no one I know will ever find it. Its evil will be diluted by time. By then my blood will be as watered down as the sea, and all my children and their children gone. Thinking of my place in eternity always makes me feel calm, a part of time with no need to fear it. It is as though all the bad things I do will *eventually* not matter. So, sitting stiffly, I ride the bike one-handed, the cold lump bumping itself against my knee.

I stop on the bridge and look around. Nobody is coming, down the road or along the cliff on the other side. Over the cliff, I can hear the rising and falling *zoOOOooom*, as cars on the interstate highway speed by. Down below me the water drives fast in its bed, the color of coffee with cream from all the rain. A dirty Clorox bottle boils by, going fast. Branches and logs and a flattened box slide underneath me, then a child's rusty red tricycle, a green plastic bucket. I reach into the pocket at last.

I hold my hand up close to my face and look at the ring in the morning light. It's gorgeous, all right. Its facets fling the sun back bent into rainbow. The diamond itself looks as yellow as the sun. The filigree is fashioned to imitate climbing vines; there are even very tiny flowers on the tendrils. It reminds me of the latticework under the porches of old houses, with morning glories or moonflowers on them, and the dark spaces beneath that store sleds and bikes and lawn mowers and croquet sets. This trellis makes an arch, support-

121

ing the gigantic diamond. I may be throwing away a fortune. Yet it is heavy, and hard, and evil. I cannot keep it.

The sound of a car brings me back to the present. I think of dropping it back in my pocket again. Surely a piece of jewelry cannot be responsible. . . . But I have to be sensible. I'm right. I figured it out, and I know I am. For even before I climbed out of the ditch day before yesterday to make my way home pushing the bike—the instant, in fact, that it crossed my mind that all this was happening *because of the ring and that I needed to get rid of it*—the wind and rain began to die down, as if to say, *You understand.* And it stopped entirely just as I got back to the house, after the quarter-mile painful walk up the steep hill. Late sunlight, pale gold, broke through the clouds like a blessing. . . .

As the car approaches, at the last second before I figure its driver can see me, before I can change my mind again, I drop the ring and immediately lose sight of it, and immediately wish for it back again. I don't see or hear the splash when it hits the water. But my finger feels free again, and I turn the bike around quickly, forgetting, until my shoulder sternly reminds me, that there is anything at all wrong. The car passes me; the woman and man wave politely. "No use crying over spilt milk," I say out loud, to print the words firmly in my brain. Never mind trite; old sayings are true.

I find Malillie having tea in the kitchen, while Treasure laps cream from a Waterford saucer on the table next to her teacup. "Hello, darling, where have you been?" she wants to know.

"Oh, just for a short ride, to see if my shoulder would put up with it," I tell her. The new glass pane still has a little square blue label in one corner. Seeing it, immediately my mind reverses gears. That was all just a bunch of accidents, caused by the storm, it says, here in the light of morning. A ring couldn't do that. And I bitterly regret having so rashly disposed of it, and wonder if I can't slip down that muddy bank, slide into the river, and search just below the bridge, in that thick water . . . I am angry at my own cleverness, for I had known I'd want to get it back, and fixed it so I couldn't.

"What's the matter, darling?" Malillie asks. "The shoulder?"

"Oh," I say. "No. It's much better. I'm—just hungry."

"I'm famished myself. What shall we have for breakfast?" and she leans on the table, her voice a conspirator's.

Bessie interrupts. "You done ate breakfast already, Miz El'ridge."

"I did?" Malillie says softly, frowning. "I don't seem to remember—"

"One egg two pieces bacon two biscuits," Bessie says. "With strawberry preserves."

"Oh, goodness," she says. "Of course I did." She sighs sadly. In the pantry the washing machine goes *sludge sludge, sludge sludge, sludge sludge*, like a heavy heartbeat. I pour a cup of tea, then make a cheese sandwich for breakfast, and then when Bessie goes upstairs I make Malillie one because she can't resist the smell of mine. "Remember how crazy you used to be about Kix?" she asks suddenly. "You wouldn't eat anything else for breakfast."

That scares me. "Oh, yes," I say. I won't tell her that she has made a mistake, that I have never liked dry cereal, that it is someone else she is thinking of.

I am still hungry, so I get some leftover biscuits and strawberry preserves and chew them in rhythm with the washing machine: *critch critch critch critch.* . . .

123

And now, without any proof, can I know for sure that I found the treasure? The explanation I dreamed was the more plausible, certainly, and sometimes seems real: at the counter, "Let me show you this," the skinny old man said, while the white cat on the sofa turned in its sleep, then curled up like a furry comma in the opposite direction. Red and green and gold embossing on the cigar box, the marbles rolling around in its smudged corners, a yellow-and-white one, a milk-of-magnesia blue one, a clear green one. And me ignoring the gold bracelet he wanted to show me, and zooming in on the ring. "That?" And him shrugging. "It's just junk. A couple of bucks, then." And the sun slanting just so into the store's dark insides. Yet when I try to remember the cave, it is like something in a book, or a place I've only dreamed about.

The ring is gone, but Malillie's birthday isn't much more than a week away. I have a feeling of urgency about that. I thought getting rid of the ring would lighten the unease I feel, the weight on my shoulders that is worse than the sprain. In fairy tales, the return of ill-gotten gains always rights things gone awry. In this case, there was no one to return the ring to (yet part of my mind contradicts me, insists otherwise): maybe, I think with reluctance, I did it all wrong, and now it is too late. I should have returned it to the pot I took it from. Too late.

And all along, through every single second, I know I am not done with the pots, as sure as God made honeysuckle.

Saturday, June 24

19

HUNTER SAYS DOUBTFULLY, "IT'S A LITTLE BIT DARK UP HERE. CAN you hold that light to the right? Can't see what I'm doing."

"I guess we could've picked a better time than ten o'clock on a rainy morning to do this." He has done the ceiling, and now we have moved to the closet that runs the length of the small room. In order to move the light I have to stand closer, just in front of where he's standing on a chair just inside the closet door. He smells clean, like soap and sun, or at least his jeans do.

"Is that better?" I ask. Maybe now is the time to tell him about what I've found.

"Yeah," he says. "I'm almost done. Maybe I ought to be a builder instead of a farmer." His voice is distorted, high up against the ceiling. I try to hold the light steady, though my arm is tired. I can't switch to the other one because my shoulder is still sore. "Then again," he continues, "if I worked indoors, I never would get a day off. I reckon the only thing worse than being a farmer would be to not be a farmer." A glob of plaster lands on my shoulder. "Except I'm so good at this," Hunter adds.

"I've heard of getting plastered," I say. "But somehow I thought it was going to be more fun than this." His chuckle causes him to bump gently against me.

My arm holding the light is really threatening to cramp. I move just a little, and in a motion I can't seem to help, I lay my head against the flank of his leg, and I can feel the movement all the way through his body of his hands and arms smoothing plaster on the closet ceiling.

Then he feels my head and gets very still. The muscle in the upper part of his leg, under my cheek, tenses, and his whole body seems to tighten. In a second he is as motionless as I am, and I can feel him look down. I close my eyes.

His hand comes to rest on my head. I don't move. I'm still holding the flashlight, and slowly I let my arm down. His hand on my head is warm. Still I stand, uncertain about what I want to happen. Briefly, I think maybe I'll wait to bring up the treasure.

In this moment I can feel the tiniest movement anywhere in Hunter's body. He has no secrets from me. He can't flick away an eyelash that I wouldn't feel.

Finally, I feel, rather than hear, him clear his throat. "Uh—we got any more plaster down there?" His voice rumbles down, strange-sounding, enclosed in the cave of the closet.

"I'll go look," I say. "I—was just resting my arm."

"Uh-uh. Stay there. Um—I mean, I need the light to see. You don't want to put any strain on that shoulder."

"But don't you need plaster?"

"No," he says.

My jaw is still against his leg, and his hand is still on my head. I guess I ought to feel silly, but I don't. "You know what you need?" he asks softly.

I don't say anything.

"A sling for that shoulder. I can rig you up one out of a necktie or an old curtain, almost anything. I one time found a deer that the mower had gotten—just a fawn. It had sheared off the flesh of both legs to the bone. But I wrapped them, and she stuck around and we fed her, and she was all right in no time."

Carefully, then, he climbs off the chair and stands looking at me in the door of the closet. His eyes are exactly on a level with mine. Greenish-blue. I swallow. Then he says, "I was thinking maybe you'd like to go to the county fair tonight over in Botetourt. Ned and them are driving over, and he said there'd be room—if I wanted to bring someone."

Someone? I think. "Ohhh—I told Graham I'd go with him. Maybe you could come with *us*—"

"No, that's okay. But don't look so sad."

"Maybe you all could split me up the middle—half with Graham, half with you."

He smiles. "If you're there, I'll find you. Uhh—listen. You"—he swallows—"ain't going steady or anything, are you, down there in Norfolk?"

"Me?" I say. "Me!"

"Yeah, you." He's grinning now.

I shake my head. "No way. I'm not engaged either. Not married, either, for that matter."

"Hmmm." He nods. Still we stand, and then he asks, frowning suspiciously, "You got any kids?"

"Kids?" I cry, too loud, laughing. "Mama won't even let us have a dog!"

"You still got my bear?"

"Well, yeah! Up in the attic. Does that count?"

"I reckon not. He's kind of adopted."

Awkward silence. "What about you?" I ask.

127

"What *about* me?" he wants to know. By now both of us are trying hard to keep straight faces.

"You engaged, married, or et cetera?"

"Nope. Well, maybe a little et cetera."

I widen my eyes to look shocked, but I can't keep my face straight.

"Actually," he says, "I'm relatively perfect. Don't drink or smoke or mess with girls. You know, just like Redford."

"Too bad," I say.

"I think we'll have to stop meeting like this," he says, poker-face.

"You mean in this closet?"

"Uh-huh," he says.

"How come? You don't like my closet? What's wrong with it?"

"I don't know." He glances up. "Nice ceiling job. But the rest of the scenery's lousy." He picks up the arm of a shirt, lets it fall.

"Well," I say, and his body is very close to mine, "I admit it's a little small, but I couldn't go anywhere else with you—like out in public, I mean."

He mugs a hurt face. "How come? I told you I'm pure of heart, no vices at all, and I look like Robert Redford—"

"You look like Will Rogers," I say, "but your face is dirty!" Now I am laughing. I swipe at the plaster streak down his cheek, but I can't pull off the gesture without my hand trembling.

"You should talk!" he shouts. "Some idiot dripped plaster in your hair!" And he puts his hand up to show me where.

Malillie appears in the door of the bedroom. "What in the world is so funny?" she wants to know. And all I can do is just lean against Hunter, and he kind of takes me in his arms,

128

or holds me up, or something, and we both shake our heads helplessly, still laughing.

20

IN BETWEEN GRAHAM AND JERRY DUNNE IN THE CAR, IT'S MY JOB to pass the rock-and-rye bottle back and forth between them. It's whiskey with rock candy in it, pungent and sweet. I had a sip at first to be sociable, but I don't much like it. Graham's cigar smoke perfumes the air. The twisty, narrow road is slick with today's rain, but when I worry aloud that we're going too fast, Graham slows down a little but says, "That Miss Sensible award has gone to your head. If I drove as slow as you'd like, we'd be September getting there." But he grins to show he's only teasing.

At first it's really fun. The rain has stopped and the sunset is deep and flame-colored. Graham asks Jerry what is the story about Henry Bergenson, and is it true he totaled the hearse? When Jerry glances at me and doesn't say anything, Graham says, "Lee's as tight-lipped as Fort Knox." And I feel a gush of pride.

So Jerry tells the story. Seems Mrs. Bergenson's husband is the guy who takes bodies to the crematorium in Roanoke when someone wants to be cremated. It takes twelve hours to burn up a corpse, so he goes to see this woman. So last week when he was in seeing her, Jerry says, this wino came along and found the empty hearse and crawled in and went to sleep. Henry came out and went back to the crematorium for the box of ashes, and headed back for Lavesia. "But somewhere on the road," Graham says, "this wino wakes up and crawls up to the front and says, 'Buddy, I need a drink,' and Henry runs off the road and wrecks. The wino wasn't hurt at all, but Henry did something to his back, and the hearse wasn't even worth pulling out of the ravine."

Graham and Jerry are laughing fit to kill, but I can't help thinking maybe it's got something to do with why Mrs. Bergenson is so awful. I tell them my story abut her and Mr. Oakley and the soda, and it's fun to have such an appreciative audience.

But then they are beginning to slur words. Once Graham swerves sharply to avoid a possum and the car scratches off the side of the road and rocks along crazily out of control until he can get it back on the blacktop. I am scared, but Jerry only breathes whiskey and says, "Whoo-ee, Graham—gonna give you this stretch along here for Christmas. Good for hand-eye coordination!"

At the fair, I walk behind Graham and Jerry to see if the rock and rye has made them wobbly. Though neither seems really drunk, both are talking and laughing loud enough that people turn to look. I really feel uncomfortable. I wish they'd hush. I watch Graham closely, but it's hard to tell if he's different or if I've just noticed, or what. I mean, he's always drunk pretty much, but it's never embarrassed me before.

A tinny calliope punches its flat tunes into the plum-color air. There's only one star out, Venus, floating low over the group of tents and twinkling lights. A farmer has obviously rented out his field to the makers of this carnival; cows moo from the distance, and the field where we've parked is knee-high in wet grass, and dangerously mole-ridden. An auction is in progress over on one side, and popping sounds echo from a shooting gallery on the other.

"We gonna go look at the cows?" asks Jerry, punching Graham in the ribs as if that were some good joke. The cattle pens are all the way to the back.

"Yeah," says Graham. "The ones in *Parisian Revue.*" He snaps his fingers. "Damn! We forgot the beer."

"Graham," I say, "there's a sign over there that says NO ALCOHOLIC BEVERAGES ALLOWED ON THE PREMISES. You can't drink here."

"Gorgeous," he says, "they just put those signs up for looks. They don't mean a thing. Come on, it's not far back to the car."

"Graham! You could get arrested," I say. I'm beginning to really wish I hadn't come.

"Ah, honey, don't be a nagger," he says.

Jerry jabs him in the ribs. "She's not a nagger, Graham! Can't you see? She's no *nagger!* She's just a skinny *white* girl!"

"That's not funny!" I say fiercely. Graham wouldn't think so either, most of the time.

I try to hush them, but Jerry and Graham giggle so at that they nearly fall in the churned-up mud of the path. Finally Graham settles down and says, putting his arm around me, "Okay, honey, we'll save the beer for later. Come on—let's get some cotton candy."

He presses a ten-dollar bill into my hand. I try for a second to remember how it's been in other years, but I can't. I seem to feel increasingly that things are different: Malillie, Hunter, now even Graham. Before, Jerry's always gone with his wife, and Graham and I have taken Malillie. "What's this for?" I ask, knowing I sound ungracious.

"You might want to buy something," Graham says. "You—might not want to do the same things we do."

I'm being paid off. I long to have come with Hunter. Reluctantly, I trail along behind them to the cotton-candy booth. I don't know how to avoid getting lost among all these people. Graham orders three cotton candies. "Not me," says Jerry. "Diabetic."

"I don't want any right now either," I say.

"Good!" says Graham. "Then I'll just eat all three of them. That was my plan anyway." He winks at me. He bites off a huge wad of the pink floss and begins to fold it into his mouth. He holds the three clouds together like they were a bunch of enormous peonies. "You know what heaven's going to be?" he says, when he can talk again. "Just clouds and clouds of cotton candy, for miles, as far as you can see. I'm going to eat my way through."

Jerry shakes his head. "No it's not," he says. "I couldn't stand that. Heaven's going to be clean sheets every night and a new insulin needle every day."

"You gonna have *shots* in heaven?" Graham asks.

Jerry laughs. "I've lived with them so long I can't even imagine an existence without them."

"I figure in heaven you can have anything you want. What do you want, baby?" And he tears off another cloud wisp and stuffs it in.

"I don't know," I say. I can never think of heaven as anything but dour-faced people wandering around in old nightshirts. A giant asylum. I hate thinking about it.

We stop near the largest tent, with exaggeratedly big-bosomed girls painted on the side, and a hawker standing outside on a little box yelling, "The most bew-tee-full girls in the whole wide world! Come inside to see sights you've never dreamed of! This way, men!"

It becomes clear that's where we're heading. Not me, I

132

think. I pull at Graham's arm. "I just decided you're right. I might not want to do what you do."

He nods, pats my shoulder. "Tell you what. Go ride the ferris wheel, why don't you? We'll come over there and meet you just as soon as the show's over. There's bingo over there, too."

"Don't worry about me," I say. "I'll be fine."

They pay quickly and go in, waving back to me. There's a flap I can't see past. I stand jostled by the crowd, in the darkening night, and feel suddenly forlorn. I think of Malillie.

We could be playing gin rummy or canasta. Eliza Triplett has come to sit with her. I wonder what they are talking about after all these years. I see them on the porch above the dripping snowball bushes, drinking iced tea, Malillie on the glider, Eliza swaying gently in the big hanging swing.

People move past me, families, couples, old men whispering together, aimless as cattle. Men stop to look at the picture of the girls and listen to the hawker, who yells the same thing over and over to each new group, drawing in one man, then three, then two, then another who glances furtively around as he goes in, as if he's scared someone will see him. Inside casbah music starts up, and the hawker cries out, "Last chance! Last chance! Come in now! The most bee-yoo-tee-full girls in the whole wide world! Come inside and see sights you've never dreamed of!"

I see a sudden arc of gold light in the dark and turn to see what it is. Off to the right is a small tent, facing the other way. I can see the light from the entrance. A faded sign, barely readable, on the side of the tent, says SEE THE HALF-MAN HALF-WOMAN! In the open back doorway of the tent a sleazy woman lounges spinelessly, outlined in the weak light coming out at the door. Moving a little closer, I can see that her makeup is heavy and hard, her hair coarse, dark red and long. She has a bare midriff, and the bra and long skirt she has on are red. She is staring out past me, into the field where we heard the cows lowing, and doesn't seem busy.

Is it possible? I move in her direction. "Is there really such a thing as half-man half-woman?" I ask. "There isn't, is there?"

"Yeah," she says.

"*Really?*" I ask.

"Yes, really." She hoists a pack of cigarettes out of her bosom, shakes one out and catches it between her darkened lips, and I realize it was a cigarette I had seen just before flicked to the ground.

"I don't see how," I say, half to myself. "I mean, I thought you *had* to be either one or the other."

"Jesus," she says, so low I can barely hear her.

For a while we stand. "How long does that girlie show last?" I ask.

She shrugs. "Maybe fifteen-twenty minutes."

I nod, but I'm not inclined to go anywhere else. I'm afraid Graham might not find me when he comes out.

"You here alone?" she finally asks. She drags deeply on the cigarette, and it lights up her face into a grotesque mask.

"No, my uncle's in there." I indicate the tent across the muddy path. "And they're just plain women," I add.

She doesn't say anything.

"I sure would love to see that half-man half-woman," I say, not liking the silence.

"They're called hermaphrodites," she says harshly.

"What?" I know I've heard that word before.

134

"Hermaphrodites," she repeats. Her voice is odd, hard. She spells it.

"Well," I say, "personally, I don't believe it's anything but a trick."

"Oh, my God," she says. She flings the cigarette out into the blackness where it makes a tiny comet of light, then lies burning a hole in the night. Then she jerks her head toward the door. "Come in here a minute." She steps back into the tent, into a kind of hall hung with canvas. There is a sour, rotten odor. I step forward unwillingly, just to the door. "Come in farther." I look past her, but no one's there. I can always run if the creature shows up. "Look, kid," she says. With her two hands she separates the draping front panels of her skirt. For a second, I don't understand. Then I see it, hanging there, heavy, protruding downward from a triangle of dark hair. Then she drops the skirt and it swings down again to hide the terrible sight. "Do you know what that was?" she asks.

All I can do is nod, then flee back, across to the lighted area in front of the girlie show to wait for Graham in the false neon light. There my legs betray me and I slump into the soft canvas against a happy dancing girl with her leg raised perpetually in the air.

"Hey!"

I ignore the voice, wishing I were anywhere else but here. I feel I've done something terribly sinful. Still the whining music grinds on, there is clapping, laughing, and then a flood of whistles, yells, catcalls.

"Hey!" The voice is nearer. Then my name. How did he (she) know my name? I begin to run, when my shoulders are grabbed from behind.

I whirl, opening my mouth to yell, to face—"Hunter!"

135

"Well, gosh," he says. "Usually girls don't run away from me quite that fast. Why, what's wrong? Are you crying?"

"Oh, it's you!" I say. "I'm so glad—"

"Well," he says. "That's better. Now what's wrong? Where's Graham?"

"In *there.*"

He looks, nods. "Oh. Well, that's nothing to cry about. He'll be back." He stops, looks at me. "Or is it something else?"

I wipe my eyes. He puts an arm around my shoulder. But I can't quit, and I shake against his side. I don't know where to begin. He says, "If you'll come on with me, I'll get you something to drink. They have homemade ice cream over here—"

"No," I say. "I'd better wait for Graham."

"Whoopee," says Hunter.

"Whoopee what?"

He only jerks his head back toward the girlie show. He offers me his handkerchief, and I wipe my eyes with it. "I'll take an old closet any day over that," he says.

And I have to laugh. "Me, too," I say. He walks me a few steps over, out of the light, and stands quietly while I try to get myself together. He's looking me up and down, and it's impossible for me to look at him. "It *is* something else," he says.

I want to tell him how everything is different, and how it scares me, and how I don't like it—

"Hunter," I say, taking a deep breath, "I've found the Beale Treasure. I mean, that's not all, but it's the beginning."

He stares at me. "You what?"

"Yes. It's true. I think I've found the Beale Treasure."

Even in the darkness I can see him frown.

136

"I'm not crazy. It's true."

He nods slowly. "If it was anybody else, I wouldn't believe them. The Beale Treasure!" he adds, his voice awed.

"See—" I begin, and I tell him the whole thing as quickly as I can, about the cave, going back, the ring, and he listens. "I'd like to take you there," I say.

At that moment, men begin to file out of the tent, looking red and sheepish. Mostly their hands are jammed in their pockets. I see Graham, taller than the rest, in the back of the group.

For a minute we wait together. Then I remember something. "Hunter. You won't tell anyone?" He shakes his head. "Not anyone. For any reason. Okay?"

He nods. "Not a soul. But I sure do want to see it."

Graham and Jerry approach. "Here she is," Jerry Dunne says. "Took up with some *boy* already. Did you ride the ferris wheel?"

"Not yet," I say. "Hunter, you know Jerry Dunne?"

"Sure thing." Hunter sticks his hand out. He still has a kind of zapped look on his face.

"Sure hope your father's feeling better," says Jerry.

"Uh—yessir."

"Well, Hunter Winfrey!" Graham says, slapping him on the back. "You following us?"

There is a sudden silence. We shift our weights, all of us. Graham says, with false enthusiasm, "Well, now! Why don't you kids go ride some rides? You're not young but once."

"Hunter," I say, "can I go home with you?" His brother's here with his family. He invited me this morning anyway.

"Hey, wait just a cotton-pickin' minute—" Graham says.

"Well, sure," says Hunter to me. "I mean, if it's okay with Mr. Eldridge."

137

Graham looks a little nonplussed. "What's this *Mr. Eldridge* stuff? I'm *Graham*, you hear?"

"Yessir," says Hunter. "I'd really like to take Lee home."

Jerry scratches his ear, and looks embarrassed. "Well—" says Graham, a little hurt, "I reckon it'll be all right." We all stand there, unsure of what to do.

Then Teddy, Hunter's nephew, hurls himself on Hunter and wants to be taken for a ride. At our backs Graham calls, "Hey, Lee! You see anything you don't recognize, just throw a hat over it!" I wave, but I'm thinking bitterly, And where were you when I needed you? In a minute he tries again, bawling across the grounds, "If you kids aren't home by next Wednesday, I'm calling the highway department!" I force my mouth up into a smile, and wave at him.

But Hunter looks at me, and he's not paying attention to Graham; instead his brow is wrinkled, and his mouth is forming the words: *the Beale Treasure!*

Sunday, June 25

21

SUNDAY AGAIN. MATCHES WON'T STRIKE. THE SALT IS ALL CAKED. Mildew smell permeates every room. It has been raining forever. Outside the color of iron lies upon everything. I have looked up the word. There *is* such a thing. *Hermaphrodite.* I don't think it'll do as word-of-the-week, somehow.

"Bessie found three mushrooms the other day growing up behind the sink, in the crack where the drainboard and splashboard come together. She said they were a sign."

"Of what?" Graham says, out of sorts.

"She didn't say."

Graham rolls his eyes.

Who *could* say? A penny in your shoe is supposed to protect you. Four-leaf clovers. Woolly bears are supposed to alert you to a harsh winter by growing their center stripes wider, according to Graham.

Once again he sits surrounded by the *New York Times.* He won't talk. Either he's guilty or angry about last night. When I asked at breakfast if he'd had a good time, he said, "Not very," and didn't ask back.

"Stop sighing," he says. "I can't concentrate on this crossword puzzle with you sighing like a cow in labor. What's a word for *treasure*, five letters, second letter is *r?*"

"Why?" I snap, feeling like someone just jumped on my back. If it would just stop raining—what? I could go back, that's what.

"Why?" Graham repeats. "*Why?*" He stares at me over his glasses, frowning. "Because it's in this crossword puzzle, that's why. What's wrong with you?"

"I don't know," I say. "I'm sorry." I want to go back to the cave. I feel the entire world has conspired to keep me from returning.

Almost immediately last night we were joined by Hunter's brother Ned, and Nancy and their other two boys, and there was not one minute to talk further to Hunter until he walked me to the door at midnight. The minute we were out of earshot, Hunter said, "How can you be sure it's really the Beale Treasure? How did you find it? Listen, I'd skip church tomorrow, but Mama'd be suspicious. How about tomorrow night?"

"I don't think we could get up there at night," I said. "It's in a little cave on Paradise Mountain. I really need you to help me decide what to do."

"We'll go just as soon as—Paradise Mountain? The Beale Treasure!"

At that moment Ned honked the horn down at the end of the drive. "I gotta go," Hunter said, close to my ear. Suddenly, leaning over, he kissed me quickly on the cheek. "My daddy always did say it's just as easy to fall in love with a rich girl as a poor girl."

Before I could think of anything to answer, he was running back to the car. Just knowing he knew made me feel better. I put my hand on the spot he'd kissed.

140

Now Graham reaches for what is probably his fourth Napoleon pastry since lunch. Powdered sugar like snow frosts the front of his gray sweater. Treasure is stretched luxuriously in Malillie's lap as she sips tea.

"I'll tell you what," Graham says, looking daggers at me, "I never thought anyone as *sensible* as you would turn out to be such a moody teenager!"

"Graham, dear," says Malillie, chiding him gently. "You won't get to heaven on other people's sins."

"It's okay," I say. "Maybe he's right." Why is she talking so slow today? She sounds like Mr. Wilshire, our drunken neighbor at home.

Now he looks at me over his glasses, frowning, and says, "Ever since you came, something's been making you broody. Like getting lost that day. That wasn't like you. Now I'm going to tell you something: I know men are supposed to be crazy about neurotic Southern women, but if you're going to start this early, it's going to be one hell of a long performance. I'm just telling you for your own good. And I'll bet I know what it is: I'll bet you're madly in love with some pimply fifteen-year-old hood back home, and he hasn't written you *once* since you got here. Right?"

"Graham," I say, suddenly furious at him, "you're crazier than a hoot owl." I stand up, biting my lips. "Listen. I need to get out. I think I'll go for a bike ride." For he has betrayed me. He's not what he was. At least he's not what I thought he was.

"In this rain?" Graham asks. "And you think *I'm* crazy?"

Malillie raises her hand in a soothing gesture. She sounds tired when she speaks. "I remember what it was like being a girl. You have *days*. You go on, darling; just be careful of that shoulder, and wrap up well."

I lean down and kiss her soft cheek. "I'm sorry, Malillie. The weather's just got me down."

She strokes Treasure and fixes a smile on me. "Don't you mind Graham," she says, trying hard, I think, to sound merry. "He's just cross because he can't fix that old stove of Harold Simmons's. I think he ought to take it to the dump." And her face broadens in a big grin, and she jiggles all over. The whole story amuses her. Seeing her laugh, I feel a little better.

Graham holds his hand out to me. "I'm sorry, too, Lee. Listen. I'm supposed to go out to Ed Corter's place to pick up some stuff Nattie wants to get rid of. Come on and go with me."

Oh, but no! Now that I'm just able to get back—"I don't think so today, thanks," I say, forcing my voice to sound casual. But I smile. "Thanks anyway. I think *trove* is the word."

"What word?"

"The word you were looking for."

"Ah," he says. "Could be. Could be. Well, I'll just finish this and go. Did you know all intellectuals love crossword puzzles?"

"Who says?"

"Sigmund Freud," he says.

"I'll bet he did."

Starting out, I blame Graham. If he weren't being such a grouch, I wouldn't feel *forced* to leave, to come out in all this rain.

With a hammer and a screwdriver banging around in the bike basket, I ride over to Hunter's and down the lane, up to the front porch. He didn't say he had anything to do this afternoon. The dog won't let me off the bike, so I holler a

142

couple of times, riding in big circles around the yard, with Wolf snapping at my heels. The truck's there, but the car's gone. Maybe they really *do* spend all day Sunday at church.

For a minute I decide I won't go back. It's chilly, and I'm miserable with water dripping down my jacket and taking forever to warm up.

But then I think, I just *have* to. So I ride carefully on the slick road, six miles on the highway, and on to 664. The air smells wonderful. And I only pass a couple of cars and maybe three trucks the whole way. Then a ways on 713. When I pass Oakley's store, I see that the old truck is parked out front, and figure that on the way home I'll stop in and say hello.

And when I get to Paradise Mountain, soaked, the bike slides, then sinks, skidding to a stop in the pitted, uneven shoulder where the weeds and summer vines are high enough now to cover the contours of ditch and road. I fall into a wet green mattress-like leaf-cloud, and getting up, reflect that I could probably not be wetter if somebody dumped me into twenty feet of water. For the millionth time, I wipe off my glasses. After today, I swear, I will never come again. I won't bring Hunter; I just want one last look, to be sure. Don't let anything happen, I pray. After today, I'll be rid of this thing, force it back into the place where dreams stay, and maybe someday tell my grandchildren that once I found a terrific treasure. I'll be happy again, after today, and stop my worrying and lying and whatever it was Graham called it—brooding. After today, I won't come back anymore, ever again. I tell myself this all the way across the field.

Yet I need to order things in a sensible manner. It was stupid, I tell myself, to have blamed a ring, a piece of stone and metal, for such mundane accidents the day of the storm. That was all my imagination. All I need is one more item. If I see them again, the pots, I think maybe I will suddenly know what to do. I didn't after all need to tell Hunter! No more after today, I keep telling myself, this is the *last time*, as I climb the muddy mountain toward the spring. There are no cattle in sight today, and the dark green leaves hang heavy with water, and bounce with the new rain.

The cave is wetter today, water dripping, I'm sure, faster than it did before; and the rocks are shiny in the flashlight's glare, slick with wet. Certainly there is more water going out of the cave, faster, making getting in harder. Could the pots dislodge? Turn over, even, pouring a stream of gold and silver out at the little basin?

I get open four of the pots, making as little noise as possible. No skeletons. No ghosts.

Bars of dull silver, black and white more than shining, fill two of the pots, rather like stacks of bricks. The smell of the pots is like blood, scary until I remind myself what I know: it is the iron in blood that gives it its odor. I must have learned that in Health.

A third pot is full of rotten leather bags on top. The first one falls to pieces from the weight of the dust, gold dust, in it, when I lift it. Gold dust sprinkles down onto the dank floor, a gentle shimmery shower in the beam of the flashlight, so I don't take out any more. I remember the day the treasure hunter came in the store, and Graham said, if you find it, bring me a handful of gold dust. But I can't. I don't even want to. Beneath the bag are irregular nuggets, looking like some dry breakfast cereal, and then sticks, or bars, of gold, untarnished. They gleam even without the flashlight. With the flashlight, they are bright and buttery-looking, the fake-gold color of daffodils. A souvenir, just a souvenir. I only want a token, some one small thing I can keep forever, some proof.

The coin is heavy, big, and very cold in my hand. But then it warms as if it has come to life. It feels bigger than a half-dollar, smooth, grainy at the edge, and heavy—heavier than anything else I have ever held. My thumb moves over the surface, and I feel whatever is stamped on it glide under. I look at it just a second with the flashlight: a head on one side, a bird clinging to a branch on the other. It's safer than a ring. Just a coin. Outside I'll look at it more closely.

For now, token in hand, I want to get away. No longer am I sure there are no ghosts.

I look for a long time at the third pot, the first one I opened. It is the one the ring came from, right on top, the first thing my hand touched. It has other jewelry. Shall I get money to help Malillie and Graham? How about Hunter: his father is sick and there's no money to hire extra farm hands. Gee and Drew? It is in my power to get Graham some help so he doesn't have to stay in the store all day, every day, year in and year out. I could maybe get Malillie to some famous big hospital somewhere for some tests, to see what's wrong. I think happily of just going through the jewelry and picking out some I can keep, or give, for presents. Maybe I ought to pack as much into my pockets now as I can, and let it go at that. A fair portion, would that be so terrible? But that time of sorting, of going through the treasure, of sifting emeralds through my fingers, which felt possible and reasonable when I wasn't right here, in the moldy cold, is not possible now that I am. I recall an old movie I saw on television: *King Solomon's Mines*. All I can remember about the movie is a chest of jewels, and a skeleton, and a man sifting jewels through his hands. I reach out several times, but always draw back.

I don't know what's stopping me. I'm thinking it's the same impulse that got me named Most Sensible, that the flip side of that is too much caution.

Maybe it's just the clammy wetness from all the rain soaking deep into the ground, dripping all around me, but my skin prickles today. I listen to the resonance of the trickling water. At any moment, something could happen: I could fall and die in here, and never be found, or—there could be retribution for disturbing the peace of things! I don't think Hunter would like it here. I feel gooseflesh grow on my arms.

I hate the thought of going back out in the rain, but inside the cave isn't much better; there is the dismal dripping all around me, all the time, which has gone on forever and will go on forever. I put the coin in an inside pocket, where it will be secure, and regretfully pick up the top of the open pot.

It slips when I replace it, making a grinding clang falling onto the pot. I wince. It feels like being in a house where there are sleeping people; you can always feel them even when there is no sound at all. I am frozen for a moment, paralyzed with fear that I might have waked something, disturbed whatever spirits guard underground treasure.

But all around me the quiet dripping goes on, like sleep-breathing, and the water burbles running out of the cave.

22

IT JUST SEEMS TOO MUCH TO BE COINCIDENCE. I CAN'T SEE HOW TO look upon *this* as an accident, finding my bike creamed into the mud bank, bent beyond use, bent beyond even walking it home, bent viciously, it seems all too clear. I can't help feeling the treasure has caused it, to get even with me for disturbing it, and to humble and chastise me for having decided

146

it had nothing to do with the other, earlier, strange occurrences.

So I stand here shaking from cold and fear, thinking it was bad luck again to take anything, to upset the balance of things hidden for a hundred and fifty years by the taking of so little as one gold coin.

I don't like to look at the bike, it is so mangled. I don't think it can ever be fixed. I should go back and return the coin right now.

And I simply cannot because all the while a part of my mind keeps telling me it was raining so hard that someone driving by just never even saw the bike, and ran over it by accident.

It's about a mile back to Mr. Oakley's store. Twice along the way I consider stopping at shacks where people obviously live, but both look as if they wouldn't have phones, though one of them has a huge television antenna standing like a sad abstract bird on the roof. It also has a faded sign in the front yard: BAD DOG. And I figure dealing with someone I know is wiser, safer. So I keep walking, the road blurring over and over from the rain on my glasses. I stumble often in the rutty, slippery mud. It feels like the longest mile in history; I seem to have walked for hours, though my watch reports that it has only been twenty-five minutes.

Soaking wet, with each step making a squishy noise, and cold to the marrow, I look forward to the comfort of the wood stove, where I'll wait for Graham to pick me up. I'll tell him I decided I just like this road—no, that won't wash—that I felt like caving, since we haven't gotten to go. I'll get a lecture, of course. But Graham's lectures are mostly hot air. And I've always gone off alone in Lavesia. It isn't like Norfolk. Sooner or later Malillie and Graham will have to know about the bike, so it might as well be sooner.

The truck isn't there now, and my heart sinks at the thought that Mr. Oakley might have closed up and gone home. HANSOM OAKLEY, PROP., the sign says on the door. NO LOITERING. MARLBORO. The door gives when I push it, protesting with the stiff sound of a spring resisting. At first I think the store is empty; then I see there are two men sitting back near the stove. As my eyes adjust and I'm able to clean my glasses, I see that one of them is Mr. Oakley. The other looks younger. I feel that I can't very well go back there now to get warm. But Mr. Oakley shows no sign of coming up front to wait on me, so after a minute I do go back to where they're sitting. Both of them watch me silently all the way.

Mr. Oakley finally speaks up. "It's you again, is it? Wet enough out there for you?" I see there are no kittens under the stove today.

"I've just done the dumbest thing," I begin, shaking the water out of my hair. It keeps on dripping down behind my ears, down my forehead, and out of my ponytail onto my back. "Could I use your phone?"

"You still got that cat?" Mr. Oakley asks. The other man just watches me, and I wish he would move, or speak, or something. I don't know what to do with myself.

"Of course!" I say, realizing at once it sounded too strong. But it was such a strange question: do people come and take kittens only to abandon them? I feel a need to elaborate: "He's growing like a weed. He's going to be a big cat. My grandmother's crazy about him. She feeds him liver and cream and sardines—"

Mr. Oakley doesn't act like he heard. He leads me back to the counter, behind a glass case of ammunition and tobacco and boxes of nails and screws, to where a greasy black table phone sits. Behind me I can still feel the other man's eyes.

The phone feels sticky and has a nasty smell. I don't like the way he stands by me, too close, breathing so I can hear him. I dial our number, thinking, Beggars can't be choosers, and let the phone ring, once, three times, six times. Where could they be? Maybe Graham's still at Ed Corter's. He and Jerry Dunne were going to dinner somewhere later, so Malillie and I would make a cheese soufflé and peach ice cream for supper, just for us. But where is Malillie?

I frown at the telephone, then find I am relieved, not having to explain to Graham where I am. There is a gun of some sort in the half-open drawer under the phone. As I look at it, Mr. Oakley snaps the drawer shut. All the time he is looking at me, and his eyes are a sort of greasy yellow-green. Even when I turn away, I can feel his eyes on my back though I stare at the wall, peeling faded green paint with pinkish-gray plaster beneath it like old flesh.

I turn and smile brightly at him. "Don't know where they could be," I say. High on the wall in back are three mounted heads: a frowsy enormous bear head, big as a sack of potatoes; a deer head with broken antlers, and a woebegone look; and a bobcat or mountain-lion head with sideburns of whitish fur, in an open-mouthed grin full of varnished teeth that look wet. The phone rings on, but by now I am sure: no one is going to answer.

Slowly I hang up. Back at the fire, the younger man sits as still as a statue, flickering red light from the stove crossing his face. Years and eons pass as Mr. Oakley moves slowly down the row of shelves and shoves some boxes aimlessly around on a dirty shelf just by my head. An ice pick is stabbed into the shelf divider above a refrigerator case with COCA-COLA barely visible through the rust on the front of it. It feels as if *they* are waiting for *my* call to be answered.

I dial Hunter's number, but it too rings and rings.

A frantic bloated fly is trapped in the glass case with the Nabs and cookies, their red bands fading.

I stand there, wet, biting my lip, trying to think, Who else? The young man sniffs and says, "How far you going," so expressionless that at first I am not certain he means me.

I swallow, somehow unwilling to say. I hesitate. "Back toward town. Lavesia, I mean. My bike got wrecked, while I was—" No response. How can you finish a sentence when there is not a single flicker of interest to keep you going?

He glances at the older one, then sniffs again, without interest. "I got a truck." Acting the cool cowboy, his lips hardly moving.

"Oh," I say. He doesn't say anything else, so I say, "Are you going to town?"

"Nope. Hadn't planned to." His chair creaks slightly as he shifts his weight.

I nod. There doesn't seem to be a lot left to say. Mr. Oakley picks up a pitchfork, heads for me, then passes me, and goes on toward the back.

"I could carry you to town—" And the young man kind of slides his eyes around at me. A ride in a pickup, with a cowboy, in the rain—

I wait a minute. "Would you?" A fat water drop falls off my hair onto my hand.

Then *he* waits a minute. "For ten dollars," he says flatly.

"Ten dollars?" Cowboys are supposed to take girls places for nothing!

"Must be ten miles," he says.

"I think it's maybe eight."

Mr. Oakley has disappeared into some back room.

The young man shrugs, creaking the chair. "Eight dollars then." And he laughs, a bull snort.

"The trouble is," I say, "I haven't got any money."

In the silence, he shifts on the cane chair, and the rainpour increases outside, as if to say, You'll get no help from heaven. "You don't," he says.

"No." After a long pause, I say, "I just—was—caving, you know." My heart speeds up.

"Caving." Mr. Oakley has come back out now, seems to be studying cans of fruit and soup and baked beans and coffee on a shelf. Why does he turn and look at the young man sitting by the fire?

"I only take a flashlight. I don't even have a wallet."

He shifts back on the cane chair, then forward, then sniffs again. Leaning back, he wipes his nose with the back of his hand. A gesture of denial, somehow. He won't take me. He looks as if he'd taken lessons from the old man, the same slow, shifty movement . . .

Then I remember. What does it matter? There's so much more—it comes clear to me that the reason I took the coin is here, now. "Wait—I do have—a lucky piece I carry. Into caves." I laugh, hearing myself sound loud in the silent store. Neither joins in. I wet my lips. "Well, it *is* dangerous, you know."

I dig it out and look at it in the store's dimness. Just a coin. A face facing right. Some stars in a ring around them. "Liberty," it says. Underneath is a date, but I can't make it out. I don't feel I can examine it closer without their getting suspicious. I turn it over and glance down. A bird, something like a dinosaur with wings, sitting on a branch. Is that a wreath in its beak? Yes. No indication of how much it's worth, but it gleams with the soft luster of pure gold. "Here," and I hold it out. It feels very heavy.

He tilts his chair back down, and rises insolently, lazily. I

151

am still standing behind the counter. He takes it, looks at it, examines it closely, especially the edge. Then bites it, his yellow teeth bared like an animal's. He glances back at the stove. Mr. Oakley looks at him. He nods slowly and turns back to me. "Okay," he says. "Truck's out back." He jerks his thumb toward the back room.

"Uh—I'm Lee Eldridge," I say. "I'm staying at my grandmother's. Lillian Eldridge. It's the house at the top of the hill—I met Mr. Oakley in town one day—"

"I'm T. B. Oakley," he says.

"You—you're his *son!*" Relief floods me, washing away the real fear I was beginning to feel. The older man nods silently. I say happily, "Your father treated me to a soda in town a while back—"

He hardly seems to hear, just opens the back door. At once rain pours in.

" 'Bye, Mr. Oakley!" I call. "See you again. And thanks for the soda and—"

The door slams as I'm about to say, Treasure. This son is apparently not one for chitchat. I give a last glance to the dismal peeled sodden door a foot from my nose, and shrug. If it's silence he wants, then silence he'll get. I tighten my jacket around my neck and dash for the truck. It's the one Mr. Oakley was driving the day in town. I wonder briefly why it's parked out back now, when an hour ago, it was out front.

The springs are shot, and the ride is bumpy, and for the first time today my shoulder really begins to ache. The windshield wipers screech across the glass, back and forth. He turns on the radio, then turns it off again when he can't find music anywhere up and down the dial. "Where'd you get that coin?" he asks, as if it were back in the store instead of in his pocket.

152

I'm not ready for that. "Uh—" I hesitate. "From my grandfather," I say, realizing too late my grandfather he'd know of has been dead for years. I glance at him to see if he believes me. "He gave it to me for a good-luck piece," I say. I like the idea, a kindly white-haired gentleman patting me on the head, putting the coin in my outstretched little-girl hand.

He drives on without commenting. I move around, trying to get comfortable, sodden and sore-shouldered. Now I have no bike, and even the coin is gone. So I still have no proof. But I am free of danger.

After a while T. B. Oakley says, "Grandfather, huh—" not a question at all.

"My grandfather in Georgia," I say, ready this time. "The one *here's* been dead a long time."

But I guess that he doesn't believe me. I scratch my head and rearrange myself on the sprung seat. "I guess it brought me good luck today," I say, and it sounds too loud and cheerful. I feel unburdened. I can always go back if I need to.

He doesn't answer a thing. The rain sheets the windshield between swipes like water dumped out of a giant bucket.

23

THE HOUSE IS DARK, NOT A SINGLE LIGHT THAT I CAN SEE IN ALL this downpour, and too quiet even for a Sunday. Inside, with the rain shut out and hushed to a dull roar, I call, "Malillie?"

Not in her sitting room. Not in either the parlor or the dining room. The kitchen, then! But no, it too is as empty as a tomb. Back through the house. Passing the veranda door, I peer through it, but the rain is pouring from the downspout and running across it in sheets.

Upstairs? "Malillie?" No answer. "Graham?" Only the steady, endless gush of the rain falling and the unnatural clatter of my footsteps. And upstairs, nobody, though I check Graham's room, Malillie's room, my room, the spare room.

Graham must've taken her along to Corter's. But in this rain? I look down into the driveway, at the woodshed door that Graham uses for a garage. Closed.

A drive in all this rain? It seems unlikely. But it's the only explanation. Isn't it?

I shiver. The whole thing is creepy. The wrecked bike, my companion who wouldn't talk, now the house empty while outside rain comes down hard enough to scare Noah. My shoulder hurts. Where can they be?

A hot bath. I'm just cold. I'll soak the shoulder. By the time I get out, they'll be coming in—they probably stopped by the store for some ice cream.

While the water runs into the enormous tub I peel off layer after sodden layer of muddy things and leave them in a pile in the corner. I take off my glasses last, laying them carefully on a white shelf. I'm just stepping in, ready to relax in the hot pale-green water, when I hear the jangle of the telephone.

Grabbing a towel, I streak half-blind through the hall, down the stairs, and grab the phone, clutching at the towel to keep it from falling. "Hello?"

"Hello. Miss Eldridge? Miss Lillian Lee Eldridge?"

"Yes?"

"Miss Eldridge, I represent the Miss University Contest Nominating Committee. You've been highly recommended to us, and—"

"Hunter! I couldn't imagine—"

154

"—and we'd like to send one of our people around to discuss your coronation. You see, the judges were unanimous—"

"Hunter," I say, so happy for the company of a familiar voice, "you are crazy."

"He's a most engaging young man. Looks a bit like Robert Redford. We know you'll enjoy working with him."

"Hunter, will you quit?"

"Can't I come over?" he says. "I want to hear more about—what you were telling me last night."

"I don't know," I say. "I just got back from—well a bike ride. Malillie and Graham aren't here, and they didn't say they were going out."

"Did you say *bike ride?* Am I wrong, or isn't it pouring out?"

"I *know.* I don't know where they could be. Listen, I'll call you back as soon as they get home. Graham's going out. Maybe you can come over after supper."

"Ah," he says, "I thought you'd never ask. Nothing could have happened, could it? They wouldn't go to visit someone?"

"I just don't know," I say. "I'll talk to you later. And don't forget Malillie's party after supper Tuesday."

"I won't," he says. "And you're going to *love* being Miss Universe. It's even more exciting than being Most Sensible. See you."

"Where did you hear—" I begin, but he has hung up. The line hums and crackles until I put the receiver back on the hook.

Back in the steamy bathroom, I add some green crystals from the jar on the shelf above the tub to the already-greenish water, and watch them descend as slowly as gold dust,

155

settle on the bottom, send up bubbles, and finally, a delicate fragrance. I think about Hunter. I have to admit he's amusing.

Miss Universe lowers herself into the warm tub. With her foot, she turns on the hot water again, just a thin stream, and half-closes her eyes to watch it fall like a crystal jet into the pool beneath. She half-dozes, her long hair floating out loose on the surface of the water like lily pads, until it becomes soaked and sinks, suspended, moving gently, in the tub. A water goddess.

Half-asleep, I see the pool beneath the cave and the same clear, greenish water, and the leaves bending down over the spring. To the left there is a movement among the green shadows; my body tenses; I whirl around; no one is there.

My body finally lifts just free of the bottom, and bobs, and sinks again, bringing me back to the present. My ears are pricked to hear the sounds of Graham and Malillie returning, but there is no sound but the water inside and out.

I wish I hadn't given T. B. Oakley the coin, as it seemed to have leaped into my hand, seemed to have chosen me as much as I had chosen it. I think dreamily of those pots of gold, and they are mine, all mine.

When I finally sit up, my hair streaming against my back, the phone is ringing again. I leap out, grabbing a towel.

A crackling like witch's laughter, that same funny sound. "Hello?" I say, shivering in the dark air, though my body is relaxed to the point of sluggishness.

"Lee?" It is Graham, sounding a million miles away.

"Graham? Where are you? I was so *worried*. Where's—"

"Lee," he interrupts. "Malillie's had a stroke. A serious one. They don't know yet—"

The crackling grows, blotting out whatever else there is.

Utter terror floods me. "Graham!" I scream. "Is she okay?"

A last sound, like cloth splitting, and then a smooth hum. I jiggle the receiver. Nothing happens, but the hum continues. And suddenly in Lavesia where I have never been lonely, I am. I reach to call Hunter. Malillie! My mind tries to find her, wherever she is. Where?

Then something out of the dark dining room attacks my bare feet, sinking claws in. I scream, hearing my voice echo in the empty house. Treasure bounds off. Everything looks blurred. I am crying and shaking. I can't call anyone like this. I clutch the towel around myself, and climb the stairs weakly, clinging onto the handrail to keep from collapsing. I am trembling all over. Treasure scampers past me going up, tail high in the air, asking, *Mrew?*

PART III

For where your treasure is,
there will your heart be also.
—Matthew VI: 21

Tuesday, June 27

24

TODAY IS MALILLIE'S BIRTHDAY. I HAVE HER BIRTHDAY CAKE IN A TIN box. I made it last night. It will make her feel better. It *has* to make her feel better. She'll love it. She loves chocolate. I pray, I hope, she can eat it. I feel that there is a dry hunk of it stuck in my throat.

It's only eleven, still over an hour before we can leave. Visiting hours at the hospital in Roanoke don't begin until two and are strictly enforced in the intensive-care unit. Graham came home Sunday night, when they wouldn't let him stay with her. Hunter showed up about seven, and when I told him about Malillie he stayed until Graham came home, urging me not to worry. He made me describe the treasure, everything I could remember. I told him about the coin and Mr. Oakley and his son.

Graham went to Roanoke alone yesterday, but today I get to go with him. I figure the store's as good a place as any to wait. I couldn't beat away the sad emptiness of the house, nobody but Bessie dragging around the old Hoover. So once more in the rain, I walk down the hill carrying the cake, hunching under my rainhood. Graham's car is in front of the store, so I put the cake on the front seat before going in to wait with Graham.

As I reach to open the door of The White Elephant, the man appears out of nowhere, blocking my path, blotting out everything, all in black, grabbing my arm hard. It's T. B. Oakley.

"Jest git in and act natural. I ain't gonna hurt you. Just act natural. I got a gun. Just act natural." His rubber coat gleams wetly.

"But"—I point inside, hoping Graham will see, will come—"I—have to get my uncle, to go see my grandmother—she's real sick—"

"You ain't going anywheres with him. You going to show me where it is. I know you found it."

"Found what?" I say, hardly able to get the sounds out of my throat. Where is Graham? Nobody is on the street. Nothing but rain.

"You think we don't know who comes and goes on that road? You been there at least three-four times I know, probably more'n that. Now get in!"

One blue car goes by, windshield wipers going fast. I think of trying to signal for help, but he shoves me into the truck, on the driver's side, and on across.

"I don't know what you're talking about," I say, as he slams the door.

"I reckon you do. Lucky piece, huh? That treasure was buried in 1822, this here coin says 1803—it all figgers. Hit's a ten-dollar piece, worth near to one thousand dollars, bound to come from hit." The truck moves up a gear, painfully, his hand on the gearshift cracked, dirty in the creases. "Just relax, there, don't you try nothing; we are going to make a little trip out there and you are gonna just show me where hit is at."

162

I try to think. If I lunge for the gun, which looks like the one out of the store drawer, he'll stop me. And I haven't ever shot a gun. "My grandmother's sick," I say. "Maybe even dying. At least let me tell my uncle I'm going."

Graham will know what to do.

But Oakley isn't listening. He's talking, jerky and nervous. "My pa always knowed that treasure had to be nearby. Why else did he buy that store in 1946, I ask you. Only twenty-one at the time, he'd done served his time in the Pacific, been pore every day he breathed, took all his pay he'd saved up and bought that burned-out old store just because hit was near to the biggest unfound treasure in this whole damn country, and he didn't aim to spend the rest of his life dirt pore, nosiree. He was aiming to find hit.

"Wouldn't try that, I was you. I got a shotgun, a handgun, and I'm bigger'n you.

"My daddy never breathed a breath he didn't think on all that gold. You touch that door, yore dead. Get yore hand away from it. Year after year, all he done was look for that treasure. Funny, he used to say on stormy nights he'd see Mr. Beale, in a black hat and a silk shirt with one of them tie bows in front, and black pants for riding, and boots. Tall, handsome. Daddy figured we was sitting on that treasure, just a matter of time till we done found hit.

"He was tard all the time when I was little, always looking, didn't let a day go by. My maw she left him cause of him looking all the time, never finding nothing. She died never believing in no treasure. But he didn't let that stop him. He knowed all the time hit was there. *Somewhere.*

"I always did figure hit had to be Paradise, that we was going to find a way to it somehow through the main cave.

"Am I right? Am I?"

"I won't show it to you," I say, not very strong.

"Hell, that's what you think. You are gonna show it to me. You been in that cave half a dozen time. Listen, I done told you once, touch that door and I'll kill you.

"Beale said hit was in a cave where farmers stored their yams at. And we have been in every filthy cave in twenty-five miles. Onliest cave anywhere around that you could of done stored yams, or anything else, is in Paradise. Took someone little and skinny like you to find a way through, what I figure.

"Daddy he give up finally. Got *saved* back there a couple years ago. Said that treasure had ruint his life up to that point, and that Jesus come down one night stood at the foot of his bed told him weren't no treasure after all. Now *he* figures yore granddaddy prob'ly really *did* give you that there coin.

"But I know different. Yessir, you are gonna show me where all that gold is at, and it's gonna be Fat City from here on.

"I am gonna be rich, yessirree. See, I figure you ain't told nobody, seeing as how you always come out here by yore lonesome, so ain't nobody gonna know but me and you."

"My grandmother—" I begin.

"Yore grandmother don't know nothin'. Your uncle neither. Else they'd a been out here snoopin' around too. And my daddy *he* don't know nothin' neither. Hee, hee! If he come to like Jesus better than gold, I figure that is his business. No need to try that; that window's been stuck for years."

"I could scream," I warn, feeling stupid, but figuring I have to do something.

"Won't do you no good," he says grimly. "Scream all you want. I reckon a headache ain't too much to pay for the Beale Treasure."

The rain intensifies.

"Goddamn," he swears real low. "This windshield ain't never worked. First thing I'm getting is a new truck. And you gonna lead me to the trough."

"Then what?" I ask, my mind having just snagged onto something.

"Then I'll decide what then."

What I realize is, he thinks it is in Paradise Cave. That will give me extra time. *Oh, Malillie*, I pray, forgive me. Don't die.

I'll keep my promise. I won't go back to the treasure. I stare grimly out the truck window at the dark day.

25

IT WAS THE COIN. I NEVER TOUCHED HIM. IT HAD TO BE THE COIN that made him fall.

My legs will hardly hold me up. It feels as if my knees might at any instant just collapse backward. I cling trembling to slippery branches and try to be careful not to slip, as it is half-dark and slick as eels down under the rain-laden trees. I am wet to the skin, sodden, and my feet are numb with cold. As I pass the spot leading off to the spring, I don't stop, but whatever paths I cut in the honeysuckle are gone, grown up again. No one could suspect anyone has ever been this way.

Oh, Malillie—the preserves, the sweets, the teapots—the lavender and cocoa and cheese sandwiches! I have kept my word. I did not go back.

I'll grow up and tell the world: *leave things alone*. Again and again I shake water out of my eyes. "Once upon a time, many years ago—" I'll say. It is useless to keep wiping at my glasses. I have to get back to the store. I have to tell somebody something. He said he'd kill me. Maybe I should stop and tell Mr. Oakley. He's my friend—I think—

Well, T. B. will be okay. Sore, probably, but the rain will revive him—I just pray not too soon, as I slide six feet, land on my bottom, and pick myself up yet another time.

I know the mountainside by now, thank goodness. I imagine I can still hear his ragged breathing behind me, and keep looking back. But there isn't anything, only the thunder, way off, and the rain, which seems like it is going to fall forever, pattering onto the leaves, then down onto me. The mountain is oozing with little wet-weather creeks that break across the path in half a dozen places now. The field at the bottom is swamplike, and my shoes are underwater in the lowest part. On the road where the truck is parked, the creek is formless, out of its banks. Pretty soon the road and culvert will be flooded and no one will be able to get a car through. How will Graham and I get to Malillie? At last I am here, and jerk the truck door open.

It smells like all old cars in wet weather: doggy, leathery, sweaty. I push the glove-compartment button just like he did, and when the metal door opens, the keys fall right into my hand. I take that for a good sign. I lock both doors and peer out the window. My glasses fog immediately, and any clear seeing is impossible.

The first key my shaking hand tries is the right one! Another good sign. There are three on the chain, and I expected that the third and last one would be the right one, as it always is in stories. Quickly I wipe at my glasses.

It's been a year since I drove, but I have no choice: I have

166

to. Miraculously, I get the engine started, but when I try to put the truck in reverse, it coughs and stops.

The windows begin to fog, and I realize I'm panting. I feel terror rising in me like the water rising outside the truck. What if he comes? I reach quickly and check the doors.

There is a movement in the brush over to the left, and I hear myself gasp. I have to get hold of myself, or I will never get away. "Most Sensible," I say out loud, from between clenched teeth. And it makes me feel calmer. Through the circle my hand makes on the fogged pane, I see it is just a small tree dancing in the wind.

I take a breath, then get the truck started again, and into reverse, and let out the clutch. The truck leaps backward onto the muddy road and chokes out again. By now he'll probably be up, stumbling around, and pretty sore at me. I wish I had gotten the gun. Oh, Malillie, I suddenly think, where are you?

But I learned something on that go-round. The next time, I let the clutch out gently, slowly, grind the gear into first, and creep forward. I don't think I can possibly turn around to go tell Mr. Oakley. I'll just keep going straight ahead, and find another way home. I can't think of stopping now I've got it started, but I'll call him the minute I get home.

Once the windshield wiper is on, and the headlights, I can see enough to inch forward. I stay in low gear. At crossroads, I turn left and left and left, in which I figure is the right direction, and pretty soon there is the highway. Once there, I relax, driving that old truck through that wet midday dusk. If I'm just not too late to go with Graham to Roanoke!

I park right behind Graham's car, carefully turn off the headlights, and pull out the key. I put it back in the glove compartment right where it was.

I have to tell Graham. And I have to change my clothes.

167

The bell tinkles behind me. A woman I vaguely recognize stands looking at some lamps over against the wall past a new display of gray modular furniture. She turns and nods at me. Graham waves from behind the counter in the back; he's talking on the phone. Amy Dunne comes lumbering out of the shop dangling a copy of *Glamour* magazine. She looks at me and says, "Oh . . . hi," and turns back into the shop.

"How are you doing, dear?" the woman asks kindly.

"Fine, thanks," I say. *Graham—how is Malillie?* My heart is still pounding.

"Is all this rain ruining your summer?"

"Oh, no, ma'am, I don't mind it at all." *Oh, can't we leave?*

"Oh," she says. "Young people these days are so much more resourceful than we were. Do you like the boys?"

"Ma'am?"

"The boys." She smiles encouragingly.

"What boys?" I ask, unable to comprehend.

"Well, I—guess you like the TV. Is Mrs. Eldridge well?"

"She—"

"Lee!" Graham's voice calls impatiently. "Where have you been? I *told* you we wanted to get away by noon! Maggie, I'll let Amy here help you. Amy! Now, Maggie, you just tell Amy what we can help you with. You know my niece Lee, don't you?"

"Oh, certainly," she replies. "We were just chatting. She's grown up so fast!"

Graham's shrugging his way into his raincoat. "How does Bobby Lee like that recliner?"

"Oh, fine," Maggie says. "He won't hardly get up for dinner anymore."

"Good, good," says Graham, taking my arm.

Outside, he says, "Honey, Malillie's had another stroke. It looks bad." He opens the door.

"Oh, Graham!" is all I can say. I move the cake carefully to the backseat.

"I don't know anything else," he says.

I look at the rain sheeting down the windshield, and buckle my seat belt. This isn't the time to bring up the treasure, T. B. Oakley, all that. I put my hand on Graham's grasshopper knee; he pats it absently, then takes out his handkerchief and blows his nose.

The car is beginning to feel like a steam bath, so I struggle out of my sticky raincoat. Graham frowns, seeing for the first time my wet clothes, the streaks of mud on my legs, a long smear of dried blood where some branch got me. "Who the hell dressed you, Jack the Ripper?"

I'm thinking how to explain, when he turns around and sees the round tin box. "What's that?" he asks. "Lunch, I hope."

"It's the birthday cake," I say.

"Oh, my God," he says, sucking in his breath. He shakes his head. "They won't let her have that, honey. You don't know—"

His face is red. The lump in my throat gets bigger, and my own eyes overflow. "I called Hy," he says. I just nod.

I wait for take-out sandwiches at a drive-in place while he calls the hospital. I can see his tall form rigid in the corner phone booth and am suddenly reminded I was going to call Mr. Oakley. I guess I can't now. But actually, T. B. will probably be back at the store himself by now, trying to get warm around the wood stove. I wish I'd had a chance to tell it my way, that the *reason* he fell off the big boulder on Paradise Mountain was that he was trying to force me to show him where the Beale Treasure was.

Graham eats both sandwiches as we pass Tinker Mountain, then the entrance to Hollins College. The windshield wipers keep up a snappy rhythm as Graham starts in on the first of four big brownies.

Again and again we splash through spots where the highway is washed with water. Once a big truck zooms by us, sending up a wave of spray that almost shipwrecks us, and Graham swears.

The hospital: disinfectant smells, bathroom odor, the reek of medicine and ether. I stand in the drab green hallway where nurses walk soundlessly, listening to the far clatter of metal, waiting while Graham goes in first. Only one person at a time in the intensive-care room. On the way home, I will tell Graham the whole thing. I think I must. He'll know what to do. NO FLOWERS, the sign on the door says angrily.

The room is dark. I can hardly bear to look at Malillie, a tube running into her nose and a thinner one running into her arm, a machine like a computer overhead. She is curtained off from other beds. A nurse sits at a desk with a big screen in the middle of the room. Malillie is so silent I can't be sure she's still breathing, though there's a *blip* on the machine that must indicate she is.

Her mouth is slightly open. Her hands lie still on the crisp bedspread. I wait, not knowing what to say.

On the bedside table stands an ugly white plastic mug, out of which dangles the yellow and red tag of a teabag on a string. Malillie hates plastic, and she hates teabags. I want to cry. "Malillie," I whisper. "It's me. It's Lee. I brought your birthday cake. It's in the car. Happy birthday." It's so stupid I could bite my tongue.

Not a sign. Her eyes stay closed. I take her hand, and it feels soft and dry and cold. "Malillie," I say. "You've got to get well. Listen, I'm so sorry I lied about the ring. Remember what I told you I found?"

Then she stirs. A frown moves across her face. "Lee," she says, her voice just a whisper.

"Yes?" I whisper back.

"Your daddy—important," she says. "He doesn't mean—he named you after me because—"

"Because what?" I whisper. I wait, but she doesn't say anything else. I have to rouse her! "Malillie," I say, "I was right. I found the Beale Treasure. I really did."

I think she hasn't heard. But then she does smile, a little, slowly, sweetly, and says, "Doesn't matter. Your daddy"—she whispers painfully—"loves you. Proud of you. Never mind the rest."

"Malillie—" I say. But slowly, her smile fades.

Her eyes don't open, don't even flutter. I can see the veins in her lids, blue-green. Her lips move, thin as paper. "Nice Treasure," she whispers.

She's still thinking about the cat. Finally she mumbles, "Can't be fixed. No use in an old stove anymore."

I stare as she tries to move her mouth again, poor puckered dry lips. Her breath comes in tiny little pants.

She doesn't say anything else. The machine continues to *blip*. I look over at the nurse, but she's reading a chart. I look back down at my grandmother, and I can't see her very well, even with my glasses. She seems blurry and indistinct. I study her face, and try to connect it with Malillie. I would kiss her, but it doesn't seem to be my Malillie lying there, just a face flattened by sleep. And all the time, in the background, is the scene on the mountain, receding like a thing you look at through the wrong end of a telescope.

There's so much I need to ask. What did she mean about

171

Daddy? Did she mean Harold's stove, or did she mean herself? How could the treasure not matter?

But the nurse clears her throat, and I jump. She indicates that I must leave. Only the slow, even *blips* prove the body lying there is alive. I take the hand one last time, and hold it. Then I back toward the door. Graham is there. Quietly, he walks over and bends down and kisses the forehead, but Malillie's face is surely already gone to some other place.

In the hall, he says, "Your father's coming up. He'll get a room near the hospital. He probably won't come to Lavesia."

"You called him again?"

"Just now. He's left already. I talked to Kate. She said for you not to worry."

26

IT'S ONLY A LITTLE AFTER EIGHT. ANOTHER STORM IS BREWING UP. Will this rain ever stop? I lie on my bedspread, too tired to even undress for bed, shivering, but not willing to move to pull up a cover. How can I sleep? Will I ever sleep again? I poke Treasure awake for company and drag him onto my stomach, but he goes limp as rags, wanting only to go back to his cat-sleep.

"Lee?"

"What, Graham?"

"Honey," he says from the hall, "I'm taking a sleeping pill to try to get some sleep. There's no use wandering around all night. Tomorrow may be a rough day." Already his voice sounds slurry, abstracted, turning toward sleep. The smell of cigar smoke wafts in. "Will you be okay?"

"Oh, sure," I say. "Graham, Malillie said something today—that Daddy is proud of me. You think she was just making that up?"

"Nooo," he says slowly. "I think she's right. But you know what? It might be like that night at the fair. I knew you were right and I was drunk, and I was embarrassed that you saw it for what it was. You never did before. It *scared* me that you saw. And Hy's a lot harder on himself and other people than I am. Also, he's so sure that the black side of human nature is going to win that he's scared if he tells you he's proud of you, it'll go to your head, make you vain or something. But think about it: how could he not be proud of you?"

I swallow. "Graham," I say, "how could you all be so different? You had the same childhood."

He comes and stands in the door of my room. "Maybe so. But people are just born different. He sees you as being like me. That scares him, because he thinks I'm irresponsible. The thing is, Gorgeous, we are all what we are. You, me, him. We can't change that. I can't change that I have never loved a woman. But you and I, we accept what we are. He can't. That's the difference. When you can't accept what you are, you can't accept what other people are either. He used to tell me, 'You have to be a good hater to get along in the world.' "

After a second, he sighs. "I'm fading fast. You haven't eaten a bite that I know of all day. Go on down and get you something to eat, or you'll blow away with the next good breeze."

"Okay," I say. "Good night, Graham. Will you call me if anything—"

173

"I promise," he says. Thunder grumbles in the distance.

Through the dim hall, down the long curved cold wooden stairs into darkness, across the hall, through the black dining room and breakfast pantry I go, and into the kitchen, where the linoleum floor sticks to the bottoms of my loafers with every step.

I open the refrigerator, and light falls in a gold square on the floor. Only then do I realize I've left my glasses upstairs. Treasure appears by my foot, saying *"Mrew?"*

"So," I say softly, "it took food to wake you up, did it?" From somewhere comes low mellow music, barely audible over the rain. Bessie has left her radio on, an antique celluloid monstrosity she keeps in the corner of the kitchen. Graham says he could sell it for a hundred dollars, but Bessie won't part with it. As I bring out ginger ale, a bunch of grapes, and am rummaging for anything else that might be good, a movement or light in the back-door pane makes me turn and look.

I can't see well at all, but I have the impression of a face. I freeze, terrified—then I remember the feeling that day by the spring. Yet, instantly, I also realize I never saw a face then, so how—? Yet I've thought, ever since that day, that I saw something—a man.

I feel half-blind and helpless. I stare back into the lighted trunk of food, to stall for time to think, to blot the vision out, and pretend to continue my rummaging. It occurs to me I might be able to see better if the lights were off.

T. B. said his father saw Mr. Beale's ghost on stormy nights. Hunter swore he met a ghost. The hair on my neck begins to prickle.

Outside water pours down as if from buckets, and the thunder cracks, closer. Rolling in on top of the rain is another thunderstorm.

174

Ghost? Ghosts don't exist. I do not believe in ghosts. Yet I am all goose bumps. Oakley: he is just a simple superstitious man. But Hunter?

What to do? Okay, I instruct myself, be sensible. Just close the refrigerator door, turn on the overhead light, and confront whoever is out there. I have just been made susceptible by T. B.'s story.

From Bessie's corner, a voice replaces the music, bringing ominous reports: unprecedented rain. Four times the average rainfall for the month, eight times the average for the past week. Slowly, I close the refrigerator door, forcing my eyes to stay on the floor until the light disappears. Then, slyly, I move my eyes to look at the door pane again.

There is no one. Nothing there. Just a pane of glass sheeted with rain. Probably some strange reflection. I stand there in the dark, feeling somehow let down, and angry at myself. How could I have left my glasses upstairs? Treasure rubs against my ankle, finagling for food.

As I peer at that blank pane of glass, trying to see, the refrigerator motor muffled to a gentle purr, the voice on the radio announces that the body of a man, Thomas B. Oakley, age twenty-three, has been found where he apparently fell off a ledge and broke his neck in heavy rain on Paradise Mountain. I go stiff. A black 1964 Ford pickup truck, registered in the name of Hansom Oakley, father of the deceased, thought to be the vehicle which the younger Oakley was driving earlier in the day, has been found by police parked on Main Street in Lavesia, with the keys in the glove compartment and the windshield wipers turned on. The incident is being investigated. Police have arrested two minors for reckless driving. A fire in the warehouse of Ripe-Rite Foods of Montvale has been brought under control, and only minor damage is reported. The morning shift is not to report to duty in the

175

Southern Valley Brewery, due to water damage in the engine room. There is a flood watch for the entire southern Shenandoah Valley, including the counties of—and then more soothing music.

Still I stand there, trying to feel something, when I feel nothing. Dead? *Dead?* In fact, I can't make myself believe the word.

What should I do? I realize my hands are full of food. I'll eat. I put the ginger-ale bottle on the table and go over and turn on the light. There isn't much ginger-ale, so I drink it out of the bottle. I eat some grapes. I cut up some cheese for Treasure, but don't eat any myself. Somewhere in the corner of my brain, I know that I am refraining from having both the things I would like to have: cocoa and a cheese sandwich. For Malillie's sake? In Malillie's honor? Is it because I keep seeing that graceless plastic cup, stained inside, half-full of cold, bitter, teabag tea?

So he is dead. Is it my fault? He forced me to go, would have killed me if I had refused. It was an accident. But now what am I going to do? Will I go to jail?

Before I cut the kitchen light off, I turn on the one in the pantry, which illuminates the near end of the dining room.

I must be more edgy than I think, because I jerk violently at a figure facing me at the dark end of the parlor, which lies open beyond the dining room. For a split second I think it is the same man I saw outside, now some way gotten in, and my hand flies to my mouth. Only then do I realize it is my own face and hand reflected in the parlor mirror over the marble-top table, only a faint, watery image of myself, that my imagination has transformed into Mr. Beale's ghost. I look as pale as a real ghost, and unfamiliar to myself without my glasses. There is a loud crash of thunder outside, over the rain's roar.

But I do stop and think, See, Lee, what the imagination can do.

So I leave the dining room, trying to quiet my heart, and head for the stairs, when a noise to wake the dead blasts through the house, shattering my composure entirely. I scream. But it is only the doorbell, which rings right behind the front door, only six feet from where I'm standing. In the black of night in this still house, it is the most frightening sound I have ever heard.

Yet the second I know it is only the doorbell, my heart pounding harder than the thunder, I move in gigantic relief and without even thinking, flip on the porch light, and open the door wide.

27

"OH, MR. OAKLEY!" I CRY, RELIEF FLOODING OVER ME. "I'M SO GLAD—" But then of course I remember—was it only hours earlier? It seems another day, almost another lifetime—"Oh, you poor man!"

"You kilt Thomas Beale!" he says, staring at me with wild eyes.

And I experience yet another shock. What in the world is he talking about? His son's death has obviously done something to his mind. Thomas Beale buried his gold in 1822, so he has to have been dead at least a hundred years! "Look, please come inside," I say.

He steps toward me. "You kilt him. He wanted to find the treasure. He thought you'd done found hit."

Lightning. A few minutes before it had only been raining and windy, but now in addition great peals of thunder crack and shake the house, and behind Mr. Oakley the yard and drive appear in eerie blue-white light. I step to shut the storm out, but he grabs my arm. "Whar'd you get that coin?" he demands.

Offended, I glance down at his hand on my arm. "Listen," I say, "I don't have to—"

But he clamps his hand tighter. "Then he was right. T. B. was right."

"T. B. was right?" I repeat. Then it was an error. The radio was wrong. He is not dead.

But then I see. Of course. He'd named his son in honor of his lifelong quest. "I only wanted to close the door," I say. "Oh, Mr. Oakley, I'm so sorry about your son!"

He stares at me. "I thought I know'd every inch of that cave. You got to show me where it is." He shakes my arm. "I got to see hit before—"

A light as brilliant as a bomb, then *crack!* The sky splits right over the house. I try to pull away. "We can't go there now!"

"Now," he says grimly. "I can't wait no longer."

What comes to me is this: Malillie will die if I go there again. I promised I wouldn't.

Tears begin to roll out of his eyes. "Why did you kill Thomas Beale?"

"But I *didn't*," I say. "How could I kill him? I was just trying to get away. He was chasing me. He slipped, and fell off a big rock. I didn't know he was—I just kept running. I thought he was going to kill me."

"Thomas Beale wouldn't of hurt a fly," he says. "He was a good boy. Good job at the lumber mill." The tears keep running down, dropping on his coat, but he won't let go of my arm.

"Look," I say, "there are flood warnings on the radio. We can't—"

"I'm sorry about that," he says, looking out into the night. Then, slowly, he takes the small pistol I've seen before out of his pocket. "Here," he says, grabbing some garment off the old brass coatrack and shoving it at me.

"Okay," I say. I slide into what must be Graham's raincoat. I keep hoping Graham will awake and come downstairs. But in this storm, it's unlikely he heard even my scream or the doorbell. Glancing at Mr. Oakley in a lightning flash I can only feel sorry for him. His face is just one sad map of pain. All that really worries me is being hit by lightning. He has the gun pointing at the ground.

He stands for a second looking at me. Then he says, "I've done come this far, and I've lost my only boy, and I didn't think there was no treasure—but now I got to see it for myself. If I wait, you'd git away and I'd never see it. So that's why you got to take me there now."

And going down the walk, pelted by rain and wind, I think, he won't hurt me. Not someone he made a soda for. I'll tell him, then, and be rid of it once and for all. The more I think of it, the better an idea it seems. I can't imagine how he'll get into that opening, but I'll worry about that when I have to. I feel surprisingly peaceful, decided, resigned.

I hunch in the truck, which is beginning to feel familiar. I don't see how the world can survive this drenching damnation. Where will all this water go?

I weigh what I want to say carefully. "Mr. Oakley, it's already killed your son. You were right to decide to leave it alone. You don't realize what you're getting into." But he just peers at the road ahead through the pouring windshield. Blue flashes light up the sky violently, and thunder explodes, reverberating off the mountains.

"Hit come up out of the fog first time, out of the field where hit dips down some just before it gits steep," he says.

"What did?" I ask.

But it's as if he doesn't even hear me. "Hit stood there, and the more I tried to see what hit was, the more it seemed like I couldn't.

"First I thought hit was a cow, or I don't know, even a bear. They see bears sometimes. Not too often, but hit could be. They can stand upright.

"Then it was like hit changed, or the bottom part come out of the fog, and I seen hit was a man, or at least what looked like one. Seemed like black for the top of his head, then white where the face would of been, and then sort of black and white down below the face part, but disappearing down where the feet would of been. I called, but hit didn't move, so course then I thought hit might not be a man. Just stood, like a animal, maybe like one of them holstein cows, looking. You know how cows stare. Except it made me feel ice cold."

Twice we go through water up to the axles, fanning it out in great curved sheets away from the headlights. I am afraid each time it will flood the motor. We pass only three or four cars on the road, their headlights startling in the dark. Once I think I see a light behind us.

"When I tried to go on over to where I could see better, seemed like hit moved back so I couldn't git no closer. Then I swear I seen it was for sure a man, staring right at me, with long black hair, with a kind of black vest over a white shirt

180

with some funny lacy stuff at the top, then black pants like them horseback riders wear. Then hit come into my head didn't nobody wear clothes like that no more."

Sometimes I can't see the road at all, though I strain my eyes into the darkness trying. Every now and then I tighten the raincoat around my body, as the jolting of the truck keeps loosening the tie belt.

"Just about then, the sun come over the mountain, I reckon, 'cause I could see it like a fifty-cent piece, up high, silver-white, glowing through the fog.

"When I looked back down, it was like the sun faded him into nothin'. In just a second or two, there wasn't nothing there. I never did see him move.

"I don't know. I thought it was Beale, and I thought he was trying to tell me something. Now what else would he be telling, except about his treasure? And ever since that morning, I figured the treasure had to be somewheres nearby.

"But then, after a while, I didn't know no more. Seemed like Jesus was telling me there wasn't no treasure—that he was reminding me that there was always a bunch of holsteins grazing that field, and that what I seen wasn't no more than a cow in that fog . . ."

"Mr. Oakley," I say, "I'm so sorry you lost your son, but I didn't kill him. He just fell." He looks at me, then nods. "I guess you might say greed killed him."

For that is what I see, clear as day in the middle of this dark night. It was only wanting the treasure—no magic forces—that caused all the grief. It was *taking* stuff, or wanting to take stuff.

We are coming nearer, driving now in shallow water almost all the way. *Malillie*, I say, *rest. You've lived a long life. Graham and I love you. The time for dying just comes, and it doesn't have anything to do with finding a treasure.* Malillie doesn't belong in that strange bed in that cold place, with a plastic cup of undrinkable tea. If that has to be how she lives, then there are things worse than dying. For us all.

I feel wildly happy all of a sudden. I am going to turn this thing over to the adult world, which may know better than I what to do with it. I only hope Mr. Oakley will not get hurt anymore. I know we ought to go back and come when the weather is better, that this is not safe, not sensible. Where did I hear that fewer accidents happen in bad weather, because people drive more carefully? Twice more through the rear-view mirror I think I see far pale headlights behind us. But each time we come to a curve and they are gone. Once I am not prepared and fall heavily against the door. Who in the world would be crazy enough to be out on a night like this?

28

THE CULVERT IS AHEAD OF US, AND THE ROAD IS AWASH WITH water from the now-furious creek, impossible to tell how deep. He is finally forced to stop the truck.

But he is not going to quit. "Come *on,*" he says, and I get out of the truck, flinching at the rain but less reluctantly than I might have, for I am about to unload the terrible burden I've carried now for—how long? Not even a month. But it feels like a hundred years. I am more than ready to let it go.

He stumbles up the hill to the left of the culvert, pulling

me along. The rain lashes us with cold water. "This is the wrong way!" I scream.

"We got to go this way!" he hollers back. "It's longer, but we can git to Paradise in maybe an hour on high ground!"

"Paradise?" I repeat. We are stopped by some barbed wire. I have visions of getting electrocuted, wonder what it would be like to die of electric shock, and decide it probably would not be as bad as most deaths. I climb over, so he won't drag me, into wind and rain and thunder and underbrush and flashing darkness. He catches his coat, jerks at it, and a piece tears and dangles and flaps on the back of him like a tail. I try my best to stop him, to tell him how useless—but he yanks me to the top of the rise, the built-up railroad bed. Before and below us, the meadow we'll have to cross has turned to a lake, mirroring the lightning. The entire landscape is different, like someplace I've never been. The road where I've always parked is lake. Is the other barbed-wire fence still there? I can't see it. I search for something recognizable, and there is nothing. I blink and squint to see. Maybe if I clean my glasses—

But then I realize I don't have them. "Now I'll never see it again for sure," I say aloud, and begin to laugh, with craziness and relief and hopelessness, while water runs in rivulets down my face. I'm used to the cold by now, and it doesn't even bother me anymore. The roaring of the wind must have drowned my voice, for Mr. Oakley is just staring around him, stopped, uncertain which way to go.

Above and beyond the lake before us is something that looks like a fallen house, standing at an odd angle just at the edge of the flood-lake. Behind it, in eerie tricky lightning flashes I can see a blurry path of devastation, even stranger for being unfocused: whole trees are trampled down flat as if by angry rampaging giants, and roots claw the sky like black lightning bolts. It is, for my fuzzy vision, sort of like trying to pick out those hidden pictures in game books for children, as my eyes try to find something familiar. Could we somehow, tricked by the storm and night, have come to the wrong place?

Then comes an immense double flash of light that makes the landscape clear as day, followed by a report like cannon fire, and I see it is the huge, houselike boulder that is lying there—the one that stood directly above the spring, the one I slipped around, leaned against to catch my breath before going on, the one Thomas Beale Oakley ran blindly out onto to see where I had gone, the one he fell from, landing not ten feet in front of me, his body twitching, then subsiding. All I thought was, he was out of commission for the next few minutes, long enough for me to get away. So I'd run quickly around him and on down the mountain, slipping, falling, recovering to run again. Later, when he failed to return to the store, his father must have come and found him.

I turn, and look at the old man standing there bewildered in the rain. My heart aches for him. He has no idea what to do. I realize that the month-long soaking of the mountain loosened the boulder and sent it tumbling, crashing down, destroying everything below it. It stood directly above the spring. That meant—that means—

"There's no way to get there now," I say. "I'm really sorry." Then, for some reason, maybe just to set the record straight, or make him feel better, I add, "Mr. Oakley, the treasure's not in Paradise Cave." Behind us, down on the road, a sound over the rain; I turn and for an instant I am sure I see a light, or lights, but then all is black again, until the next lightning.

Mr. Oakley is staring at me, frowning. Water is pouring off him, and dripping from his eyebrows and nose and ears and chin. "Not in Paradise?" he echoes.

I shake my head. "No. Not in Paradise. It never was."

His face grows more puzzled than ever. I point toward the boulder across the field. He mumbles something I can't hear. "What?" I say.

Then he says loudly, "I said I never did think it was."

"That's right," I say, nodding, and start to explain. "It—"

But at that second he turns his face upward to the drenching sky and cries, "Lord Jesus! Hit ain't there!"

Water bounces off his face, runs down his neck. He stands, eyes closed, his face taking the rain. "I knowed it. I knowed it!" he says. He seems to have forgotten all about me. I clutch Graham's wet raincoat tighter around me. Lightning flashes, flashes again, off toward the south. The main strength of the storm is past us, going fast away.

Is he okay? I tug at his arm. "Mr. Oakley—"

He opens his eyes and looks at me. "Miss Eldridge," he says, "I am just a crazy old man. Bringing you out in the night for nothing. You should of told me. And that coin wasn't nothing but a good-luck piece after all. Well, I'll be damned."

What is he talking about? I must be gaping in my confusion. He turns abruptly and starts back down to the road where the truck is, his shoulders drooping and dripping, his coat flapping crazily.

What did I say? I can't remember. After a few seconds, he stops, turns around, and hollers at me, "Come on. Come on here! You'll catch your death. We got to git out of this goldarned rain!"

And I tear down the hill, knowing only that somehow, the ordeal is over. I don't know how, but I'm willing to believe in magic.

29

CAN IT BE THE RAIN IS STOPPING? FOR GOOD, OR JUST AGAIN? AS I
walk up the path I stare upward, but the sky is just sodden
tarp. The house stands blurred, silent, dark, except for the
lone porch light, a fuzzy green-gold glow. Without the
people who belong in them, houses have no life. It comforts
me to know that Graham is asleep there anyway. I try to think
about Malillie, but it's as if she's already become a part of my
childhood, my past. I know she can't recover, and with teabags and tubes the only possible future, she wouldn't want
to. She was right: the only thing to do is to throw out an old
stove. I wouldn't want her to stay alive in those circum-
stances.

I look back at the indistinct path down to the road, thinking I hear a car over the sounds of rain and gushing water.
The truck is long gone. Mr. Oakley isn't big on the amenities,
apparently figured I could make it to the door on my own.
Around me rain drips and drizzles, a million drops from the
tall oaks, an instant shower when the wind stirs the leaves. I
imagine that, a mile down the hill, I can hear Rough Creek
tearing through its channel. Sounds seem very clear; only the
sights are blurred. A truck horn hoots in the night, far away,
out on the interstate, a mile or more. But then, over all the
natural sounds, I hear one that terrifies me: the tiny metallic
click of a car door shutting.

Panicked, peering over my shoulder, I bound onto the
porch. It's him—he's come back—he—I *know* I can hear footsteps on the gravel!

The doorknob is stuck, the door swollen like everything else by wetness! As I struggle with it, desperately, I hear heavy footsteps inside, then it jerks away from my hand.

"Daddy!" I cry, in relief. I never think about what he's doing here at this hour.

"You!" He strides out onto the porch, angry, raking his fingers through his hair.

I reach to give him a hug, and feel him, as always, stiffen. "Where in God's name have you been?" he roars. "And why the hell haven't you got your glasses on?"

Once more I look over my shoulder, into the blurred night. But it must have been my imagination working overtime again. There's no one there. I look back at him. His hair is messed up, and his eyes—"Running around in rain like this! You must be crazy!"

Suddenly all my energy is gone. I feel so tired I don't think I can stand up any longer. I'm not up to a confrontation, a fight, accusations. I feel tears welling up behind my eyes. "How's Malillie?" I ask softly.

Perhaps mad about being done out of a fight, he glares angrily at me, turns, paces the porch, addressing the darkness beyond it. "I have *never* driven in such rain! There are floods in five counties! Including this one. I drive like Jehu to get to the hospital. And find no one there! So I risk life and limb to get *here*. And arrive to find Graham *passed out*, too drunk to even wake up! And you not even here. Gone! Gone God knows where, somewhere out in all this! And with God knows whom!" He waves his arms like a preacher. Sometimes when he does this at home, the neighbors come out to listen. I'm grateful that at least here we don't have any. Abruptly, he turns back on me again. "What the *hell* was I supposed to think?"

I close my eyes and try to keep from crying. He's just scared, he's upset, he feels alone. He can't even let himself admit how worried he is about his mother.

I turn, thinking to say some of this—

But someone *is* coming. This time the crunch of feet on gravel is clear. "Lee!" I look out, puzzled, into the dark yard, unable to see more than a few feet because of the porch light. That was *Hunter's* voice!

"I nearly forgot," he says cheerfully, moving into the light. "I'll ask the warden to open the church in the morning to see if we can find your glasses." I am sure my jaw is hanging loose as he bounds past me, up the porch steps, and shakes my father's hand vigorously. "Why Mr. Eldridge, sir! Did you just get here? What a night to drive!" Then he stands there grinning innocently.

"Why, uh—yes," says Daddy, his ruffled feathers subsiding already. "Yes, indeed it is. So you kids have been to church, have you?" He's still gruff, but now definitely on the defensive.

"Oh yes *sir*." Hunter nods. "Our youth group. But I was anxious to get Lee home *early*. You know, this weather!" And his broad gesture takes in yard, sky, earth.

"Well, you scared me to death," he says, but now his voice has regained its normal level. "I had no idea where Lee was."

Scared. Had he ever said it before, and I not heard? Well, it wasn't much, but it was something. I tell myself Rome wasn't built in a day, and all that. I'll remember.

Daddy gruffles a bit, trying to regain his dignity. "Are you old enough to drive?" Daddy asks Hunter sharply.

"Well, sir," and Hunter actually shuffles his feet a little, grins, then scratches his head, "I've *known* how to drive for several years, and my parents let me drive around the farm

188

and all, but of course I'd never have driven with anyone else in the car if the weather had been even half-decent. The church is less than a mile away, sir, and I drove real slow." He ought to get an Oscar for this one.

My father glances at me, which gives me a chance to nod vigorously in agreement. He nods. It's okay.

A small pause . . .

"Well, good night, sir," Hunter says. "G'night, Lee!" And, waving, he disappears again into the darkness, whistling.

I can't believe it. I am still stunned. I can't make it out at all.

But, beat as I am, there is something else . . . "By the way," I say, "Graham took a sleeping pill so he could get some sleep. He hasn't slept for days. He isn't drunk. We went to see Malillie today. We're going again tomorrow."

He nods, as if half-hearing. Then he says, "Honey, Malillie died a couple of hours ago."

Wednesday, June 28

30

I GRAB HUNTER AND LEAD HIM TO THE KITCHEN SO FAST HE'S STILL holding onto the coconut cake they've brought. "I'm really sorry about Miss Lillie," he starts. His mother and father are standing in the hall with a pie covered in tin foil and a huge jar of vegetable soup. The kitchen table is already full of food. I push some things closer together to make room for the cake.

"Thank you," I say, taking it from him. "Me, too."

I stand, staring down at her table, her kitchen. And she's not here, never will be. But then I remember. "Hunter," I say, "how in the world did you *manage* that?"

"Manage what?" he asks innocently.

I shake his arm. "You know what!"

He grins. "Just part of my Redford complex, I reckon. What are you doing with your glasses on? I was supposed to bring 'em back."

And it's my turn to grin. "I have two pairs. I suppose the warden found the others?"

"Oh, sure," he says. "Right where you dropped them, in the punch bowl. Tsk tsk!"

"Hunter!" I warn.

"Okay, okay," he says. He takes a deep breath. "I came at eight for Miss Lillie's birthday party," he says. "I *was* invited, if you recall. Then when I drove up and saw you getting in a truck with a strange man, I couldn't think what you were doing. Then I figured it must be Oakley. I don't know why y'all didn't see me. I was going to step in, see what was going on, and then I got a glimpse of the gun, and I didn't know what to do but follow you. The only hard part was driving with no headlights. Couple of times, I about drove off the road."

I nod slowly. "And every now and then you had to switch them on for a little bit."

"You saw?"

"Well, I kept *thinking* I saw headlights. Hunter, I just realized, Malillie died on her birthday." I must look sad, because he puts his hands on my shoulders. "And you were along the whole time!"

"Well," he says, "I wanted to see the treasure! Also, I was hoping to get a chance to rescue the girl. Redford always does."

"You rescued me, all right," I say. "But how did you know to come up to the porch?"

"That was luck," he says. "I was going to check on you after the old geezer left, and I wasn't sure how to do it without scaring you to death. But then your Dad showed up, and he sounded pretty mad—and you did tell me nobody could know about the trea—"

"Shhh. Right," I say, putting a silencing finger on his lips. They are very soft, so I kind of leave it there. "Hunter, it got buried in the landslide. The whole mountainside's washed out. I'll never find it now."

Behind my finger he smiles. "A likely story."

"But it's *true!*" I protest.

Hunter moves my hand with his hand. "I know," he says. "I heard on the radio. But it's better this way. Don't you know what the Bible says? 'Lay not up for yourselves treasures upon Earth, where moth and dust doth corrupt, and where thieves break through and steal—' "

He breaks off suddenly, and kisses me for real. And when he's done, he says, "You can open your eyes now."

And so I do.

"What are you grinning about?" he asks. "That was just for if I don't get to see you for a while."

I look down. I really can't go back. "Hunter," I say, "someday I would like to tell people the truth. At least Daddy. I mean, I think he'd really be interested."

"Then someday you will," he says. "Come on, or they'll wonder what we're up to out here."

Friday, June 30

31

" 'WE BROUGHT NOTHING INTO THIS WORLD, AND IT IS CERTAIN WE can carry nothing out. The Lord giveth, and the Lord taketh away . . .' "

Sitting there with the hot sunshine on my head, under a sky as blue as the sea, it is hard to imagine the way it was only three days ago, the world dark, the power of water everywhere. Now there seems only peace, the sifting of light wind through the lush shining greenery that crowds up to the edge of the cemetery, standing on the outskirts of town, the land cleared only a hundred feet or so back from the raw rectangle cut out in front of me. The earth from it is piled up in a ragged cone. Daddy sits stiffly on my left in the row of gray metal folding chairs, Drew is leaning into my lap, and Graham is on my right holding my hand so hard it hurts. The minister reads the only service that Graham thought Malillie would have found tolerable: Episcopal. No church, no choir: only the return to nature of nature's used parts. Like the stove. Drew looks up at me, asks, "Lee, what's heaven anyway?"

I hug him tight and whisper, "Shhh. This is a time for listening. We'll *talk* about it later, okay?"

" 'The days of our age are threescore years and ten; and though men be so strong that they come to fourscore years, yet is their strength then but labour and sorrow; so soon passeth it away and we are gone.' " The minister pauses. Malillie got five extra years. I think how wise the words are: it was time for her to go.

Graham says maybe he'll close up the house and go to New York. When I worried, he told me, "I'll be selling Forty-fourth Street to the natives in a week. You'll come visit. There are lots of Southerners in New York."

Yesterday and today, with Mama and Gee and Drew, the house has felt full of life again, the boys fighting, Gee complaining to me, "Lee, make Drew color in the lines. He won't color in the lines, and it's my book!"

And Andrew looked up from the dining room floor and smiled peacefully at me. "I think it looks nicer out of the lines."

I leaned over and grabbed one with each arm and hugged. "I love you both," I said. "Don't fight today, okay?"

This dress Mama has brought, stiff and dark blue and uncomfortable, chews at my waist. But I suppose funerals were not meant to be comfortable. I've fixed a box for the trip home for Treasure. Drew has already adopted him. I've packed the Cantonese teapot from Malillie's collection that I chose, the white one with orange dragons and gold edging, and vines of light green. I chose it only at Graham's insistence that Malillie would have wanted me to have it. Somehow I know that is true. The rest, my clothes, will take two minutes.

" 'In my Father's house are many mansions,' " intones the minister. " 'If it were not so, I would have told you.' " I like that, for it seems to mean that for good people, many kinds of lives are possible. Beyond that I can't say, but it pleases me

194

because I know that Malillie's religion was an intensely personal thing, not to be confined in a church.

My mind drifts. Someday I will tell Daddy about finding the Beale Treasure. But not now. Maybe never. Because now, I know what he'd say:

"That's the most ridiculous thing I've ever heard. Now you can't expect me to believe—you've been here with Graham all this time, upset by Mother's illness—"

Then I'd have to protest: "But I *did*," with no proof.

Because the next thing he'd say: "I reckon you walked away without taking so much as a single nugget, did you?" And he'd go on: "People have claimed for years to know where the Beale Treasure is. But you notice ain't none of them rich. A man on television recently claimed to have it figured out, said he was going to bring it out when the time was right, when taxes were more favorable. Likely story." It would be another one of his retribution stories.

Graham would probably believe me. He'd catch my eye and wink and say something like, "Dogs love to chase cars, but what would one do if he ever caught one? Who'd believe him, especially if he didn't bring the car back with him?"

And Daddy would retort, "Who the hell said anything about dogs?"

And then Graham, leaning back and balancing his chair dangerously on two legs, which Daddy hates, would say, "So my smart niece has finally found what everyone's been looking for all these years! I'll be damned. Now tell us exactly where it is. Twenty-five words or less!"

That's how it would go, the story spreading from Graham to Jerry Dunne, and so on, like an autumn brushfire, until it was on everyone's tongue in the town, and I'd never have an easy moment here again.

But suddenly a movement on my left startles me back to

awareness. Daddy is crying, his shoulders shaking violently. I
have never seen him cry before. At the same moment that I
notice, I become aware that Mama, on his other side, has
noticed. I look down. His hand is clenched at his side, and all
I have to do is reach, and take it. So I do, cautiously. At first
he keeps it stiff, but then, in a minute, his hand relaxes, and
he rubs the back of my hand with his thumb.

What if I could do it all over, this month?

Maybe I'd never go back for the second time, never touch
the treasure, but instead just keep the blessed uncertainty of
my eyes.

Or maybe I'd tell right away, starting with Graham, and
have it out of my hands and off my conscience. I'd lead them
to it, and stand and watch them bring it all out, with the big
machines and the television cameras, or whatever, and maybe
be written up for a harmless moment of glory by the Roanoke *Times*: THIRTEEN-YEAR-OLD STUMBLES ONTO
FABULOUS BEALE TREASURE. Maybe I'd even get a pair
of gold earrings for a token.

That might have been the best way. It wouldn't have
changed a thing about Malillie, but it might have been the
best way.

I wish I did have some proof, just some tiny thing.

But all in all, I find I am satisfied to have it buried again,
still hidden. A mystery should stay a mystery, if you ask
me.

Across from us, at the back of the crowd, stands Mr. Oakley, in a shiny navy suit, his hat in his hand, staring down at
the ground. Seeing him, it strikes me with shame that I never
heard about T. B.'s funeral, never even thought about it.

" 'Lay not up for yourselves treasures upon Earth, where
moth and rust doth corrupt, and where thieves break through

and steal. But lay up for yourselves treasures in Heaven, where neither moth nor rust doth corrupt and where thieves do not break through nor steal. For where your treasure is, there will your heart be also.' " The minister continues. "And now from Saint Luke: 'Lord, now lettest thou thy servant depart in peace . . . ' " I look around at Hunter, behind us. I catch his eye, and he gives me a slow sidelong smile.

The rich polished wooden coffin is covered with red and white roses long since gone wild in our garden. I feel peaceful more than sorrowful. Staring down at my feet, I see a four-leaf clover and lean to pick it up. It is real. I remember how someone told me once that in those laminated plastic cards they aren't real, just regular three-leaf clovers with an extra leaf added.

Hunter is standing in the back behind me, in his dark blue suit, with his parents, and Eugene, and Ned.

When the wind ruffles the trees, I can smell summer coming at last, rich and green and earthy. It looks as if the rains are over. It was the worst flood in nearly forty years, with road damage and mud slides all over the county. It will still be a while before the water gets back to normal and the people in the low-lying parts of the area get the mud out of their houses.

Suddenly my eyes catch a movement at the very edge of the woods where light green grass stops and dark trees begin: some trick of sight, for I thought, for an instant, that someone stood there: Malillie! I nearly shout her name, but as my mind catches up with my heart, I know it could certainly not have been Malillie with her white nightdress flapping gently in the breeze, as I for an instant thought.

" 'Therefore will we not fear, though the earth be moved and though the hills be carried into the midst of the sea, though the waters thereof rage and swell, and though the mountains shake at the tempest of the same.' "

I have the clearest sensation that Malillie—the figure standing there—is directing me to listen, listen carefully, to the words the minister is saying. And in that instant, the minister pauses, and lifts his head for just a second, toward the same spot. I look toward it and smile. But there is only the early afternoon dappling, hard light on green leaves, soft spots of sunlight falling, patches of lighter green, a breeze caught in some branches, layers of green. Only my imagination: there is nobody there.

He is finishing, his hands tracing the shape of a cross in the air. " 'Our Father, who hast set a restlessness in our hearts, and made us seekers after that which we can never find . . .' "

I look at the minister again. He raises his eyes and smiles directly at me, then finishes the prayer. He steps forward, picks up a handful of earth from the dirt pile by the grave. "Unto Almighty God we commend the spirit of our sister Lillian Lee Eldridge departed this life, and we commit her body to the ground: earth to earth, ashes to ashes, dust to dust . . ."

Afterward, the breaking, scattering, milling: Daddy blows his nose once, hard, and is again his own self, made of stern stuff. Yet I have seen just for a moment underneath: if there is more, I can find it. They file by to nod or shake hands or mumble condolences, to Graham mostly, to Daddy, to me: among them are Bessie and several of her kin, Mr. Fox and his tiny gray-haired wife named Lois; Jerry Dunne and his plump dimpled wife, wearing a pink satiny-looking suit. Here is Eliza Triplett, frail, on the arm of her son Walter, who talks to Daddy and says something to make him laugh. Dr. and

Mrs. Carter. Hunter's parents. Even Mrs. Bergenson. Mr. Simmons and his wife Norma, not nearly as interesting-looking as I had somehow imagined. Others. Most I recognize. A few I don't.

Toward the end, Mr. Oakley comes. He says, "I'm real sorry about your grandmother."

"Thanks," I say. "And I'm sorry about your son."

He nods, wipes his eye, but doesn't seem inclined to move on yet. Daddy talks to an old friend. Mama talks to an old woman, then leads Green and Andrew down a row of old headstones to show them something on a tombstone. Graham is talking to Mrs. Triplett and another old lady. It is almost over. The sun feels hot on my head. Suddenly Daddy laughs. "That your father?" Mr. Oakley asks.

I nod.

He rubs his nose with the back of his hand and shuffles his feet restlessly, uncomfortable in his good suit, but still in his mud-caked boots. "Reckon I'm a crazy old man," he offers. He sniffs and looks at the sky. "They saying Paradise Cave's filled with mud. Collapsed from inside. Whole dang mountain collapsed." I nod again. "Hit's going to take the highway department a piece of time to dig that road out. Reckon I won't be gitting much business for a while. Ought to go to Florida."

"That'd be nice," I say.

He turns away, still clutching his hat, then turns back again. "I *told* T. B. you never found no treasure," he says, "but he was hell-bent you did. Reckon Thomas Beale's still guarding it somewhere. The one hid it, I mean." After a minute he says, "Maybe T. B.'s guarding it too, now." I glance over to the right, and Hunter is there, standing. He's waiting, I think, in case I need him again.

Over by some tall trees Drew gives an Indian whoop. Mama shushes him, and takes him by the hand. She stoops down to tell him something. Mr. Oakley shakes his head, and examines the brim of his hat, turning it slow and deliberate in his hands, frowning, "Hell, ain't no Beale Treasure. I'm crazy, is all."

I feel so sorry for him that I say, "Mr. Oakley, you're not crazy. I believe you—you know?—about the ghost? The night of the flood, before you came? I saw it too. I don't know which T. B. it was, but just for a second I thought I saw his face, and kind of funny clothes—just like you said. Of course, I know it was only my imagination—"

He chews his lower lip for what seems a long time, and I edge over in Hunter's direction, anxious to talk with him before we leave. Mr. Oakley stares up at the sky with his yellow-green eyes, before looking back at me. "I'm right where I was when I started, only I'm forty years older. I done wasted my whole life. You believe in ghosts?"

"I don't know," I say. I watch Daddy walking through the cemetery now toward Mama. And way off, Mama and Gee are still walking slowly, reading gravestones. Outside the iron fence, cars start up, drive off. Graham stands directing the caretaker, who shovels dirt into the hole. I take off my glasses and wipe them on the hem of my dress, and it seems Malillie is somewhere here, laughing, saying, Throw out that old stove. Get a new one! Only just not able to talk.

Mr. Oakley still stands, not finished. Beyond him, I see Drew leapfrog over two small tombstones. "I think T. B. done run over your bike," he says. "I'd—like to git you a new one." He rubs his nose vigorously. Before I can reply, he goes on. "Look. Maybe it weren't no ghost the night T. B. died, at your kitchen window? A man can get crazy with grief."

He said *kitchen*. What I can't remember is whether I said it to him. But his truck was out front, the lights were all off in the house, and how could he have known where I was going to be at exactly the moment I opened the refrigerator door?

Hunter moves a little bit closer, looks at his watch. "Mr. Oakley," I say, "thank you for coming—"

"You going home to Norfolk?"

I nod. "At least for the time being."

"You come back now," he says. "I got no kid now—but you. I mean to give you back yore good-luck piece. But I don't know where T. B. put it."

"It's okay," I say. "I have—the cat." I think about Treasure, sure to be miffed at being imprisoned, and to complain all the way home. He's my only souvenir. The ring, gone. The coin, gone. Somehow, miraculously, Mr. Oakley doesn't know I've found anything. And I might as well not have. Not a shard of evidence.

"The Lord knows a thing like that can ruin a man's life, turn him from goodness, doom his soul," he says. "You take care, you hear?"

"You, too," I say. Gee has disappeared high into the huge magnolia tree in back of the shed-cottage in the front of the cemetery. Drew stands at the bottom whacking the tree with a stick and imploring him to come down. He drops the stick and comes running across the grass to me, zigzagging through the rows of headstones. Hunter ambles toward me.

At the edge of the cemetery, in the small line of cars, the streaked black truck stands apart, as if it knows its place. Mr. Oakley walks stiffly toward it, not looking back.

"Lee!" It's Daddy.

Hunter turns to look as I wave.

"Oh, Hunter," I say, "Daddy's wanting to go." Drew

appears now and leans against me, wanting to be picked up. It's time for his nap. I hoist him to my shoulder. "Leee-eee-eee," he drones softly, his head flopping.

Hunter watches this. "Miss Lillie was one of the finest ladies I ever knew," he says. Then he swallows with difficulty. That's not what he's come to say. "Listen, now." He stares at the ground. "Couldn't you maybe write me a letter sometime?"

"Maybe I could," I say, over Drew's head, smiling, kidding him, holding back.

"You better," he says. "The Lord knows what would happen to you without me to look after you."

"That's true," I say, smiling, thinking, Hunter listens to even the things I don't say. "Really, thanks."

"Lee! It's time—" Daddy calls again. I wave again, nodding.

"If you forget to come back, I'll just have to come get you," he says. "Reckon I could find my way to Norfolk."

"You just head east and start walking. Nothing to it."

"Leeeeee, I lo-oooove you-ooo," Drew croons. Hunter looks at him and smiles a secret smile.

And then we both don't know what else to say, so we grin at each other and he reaches out his hand, and I reach out mine, but Drew is too heavy, and I miss his hand, and we laugh, and for now I have to just let him go.

Lugging Drew, I walk over to where Graham stands looking at the grave. Everyone is gone but Jerry Dunne and his wife. Mama and Daddy and Gee are waiting over near the gate. Jerry Dunne's arms are around Graham's shoulders.

I smile at Mrs. Dunne, leaning backward with my dead load. Jerry's wife, smiling encouragingly, clutches her small white pocketbook in both hands. "Isn't he darling . . ." she murmurs.

"I want Mama," Drew sighs.

"I'll be back," I tell Mrs. Dunne. I heave Drew up higher on my shoulder.

I reach Mama and Daddy and Gee. Daddy frowns across the cemetery at something that he doesn't like. "Downright embarrassing," he mutters. "That morphodyke."

What *is* he talking about? I peer back over my shoulder. What he's looking at is Jerry and Graham hugging each other.

And suddenly I know what he means, and have to stifle wild laughter. Or is it a flood of tears?

Sniffling, I am glad of something to do, and pass Drew to Mama. He is sound asleep now, ragdoll limp. He lets out a little snore, and I have an excuse to laugh. "I want to tell Graham good-bye," I say.

Passing the headstones, wooden, falling-down, stone, weathered or new, polished or pocked, mounded or sunk into the dirt, I feel tremendous pity for Daddy. I am embarrassed for him that he doesn't even know the words for the things that he is frightened of. And I know Graham is right: he's scared of so many things.

Mrs. Dunne is smiling, nodding sympathetically at Jerry and Graham. "They're such good friends," she says. "It's such a blessing." She has dimples.

I close my eyes for a second to rest them. I open them again, and nothing has changed. I take off my glasses and rub my eyes with my free hand.

Mrs. Dunne mistakes my action for grief. Awkwardly she reaches out and pats my shoulder. "It's all right, honey," she says.

I nod. "Yes," I agree, watching the two men until Graham turns to hug me good-bye.

Author's Note

Katie Letcher Lyle attended Virginia public schools, obtained her B.A. degree from Hollins College, and her M.A. from Johns Hopkins University. She has taught English and humanities at Southern Seminary Junior College, Buena Vista, Virginia, since 1963, has written a weekly food column for the *Roanoke Times*, and is the author of many poems, book reviews, and articles on a wide range of subjects, as well as four earlier novels for young adults, including *Dark But Full of Diamonds*, published in 1981.

Mrs. Lyle has been a professional folksinger and an amateur actress, and has lectured widely on young adult literature. She lives with her husband Royster and their two children, Cochran and Jennie, in Lexington, Virginia.